CROSSING THE TEES

THE FIRST SHORT STORY ANTHOLOGY

6e

Published in paperback in 2018 by Sixth Element Publishing
on behalf of Crossing The Tees Book Festival

Sixth Element Publishing
Arthur Robinson House
13-14 The Green
Billingham TS23 1EU
Tel: 01642 360253
www.6epublishing.net

© Crossing The Tees Book Festival 2018

ISBN 978-1-912218-22-6

British Library Cataloguing in Publication Data. A catalogue record for this book is available from the British Library.

All rights reserved. No part of this publication may be reproduced, stored in a retrieval system or transmitted, in any form or by any means, electronic, mechanical, photocopying, recording and/or otherwise without the prior written permission of the publishers. This book may not be lent, resold, hired out or disposed of by way of trade in any form, binding or cover other than that in which it is published without the prior written consent of the publishers.

The authors assert the moral right to be identified as the author of this work.

Printed in Great Britain.

This work is entirely a work of fiction. The names, characters, organisations, places, events and incidents portrayed are either products of the author's imagination or used in a fictitious manner. Any resemblance to actual persons, living or dead, or actual events is purely coincidental.

CONTENTS

Foreword by Tracey Iceton, Writer in Residence....................1

Winner
Michael Parker - Slagheap..3

Second Place
Colin O'Cahan - A Crossing 13

Third Place
Ethel Stirman - Beyond The Bridge 19

Highly Commended
Marianne Amy - Sometimes The Gods Collude With Us 31
Ann Cuthbert - Of Gods And Goats......................................43
YD Jones - Alice And George 55
Chitra Kumari - Crossing The Tees 69

Shortlisted Finalists

Michael Atkinson - A Bridge Between Strangers 75
Julie Baggott - La Question Francaise 87
Sue Baxter - The Page With Nothing On It 97
S.A Boon - Making Waves 101
Jane Bradley - Maggie 113
Sue Campbell - The Shopkeeper 121
Rachel Camsell - Restoration River 133
Arthur Duncan - The Bridge 137
Paul R Jasper - Stung 151
Tricia Lowther - What Remains Of Roger 165
Geoffrey Marsh - The Triumph Herald 171
Peter Martin - Girl In The Water 185
Sue Miller - Minding The Gap 197
David A Murray - To King And Country 207
Paul O'Neill - Jimmy Jesus 217
Janet Philo - Blue Bridge Crossing 227
Alan Pilkington - Water Under The Bridge 231
Kelly Rose - Ice Cream Tees 237
Jacqueline Saville - Ghost Bridge 247
David Smith - Graphite 251
Alan Theakston - Water Under The Bridge 253
Ian Todd - Our Bridge 263
Emily Willis - Pointed And Precious 265
David Willock - The Skirmish At Yarm 277

Writer in Residence

Tracey Iceton - Eclipsed 289

FOREWORD
TRACEY ICETON, WRITER IN RESIDENCE

When people think of the North East, the Tees Valley in particular, minds might turn to the steel industry and the railways, to working class culture generally. They perhaps less often associate the region with literary creativity but a wealth of talented writers call Teesside home, as this anthology proves.

As an author proud of her northern roots, I was delighted to be offered the chance to work with emerging local writers as part of the 2017 Crossing the Tees Book Festival, the year the festival launched its first short story competition. My writer-in-residence role focused on helping writers produce quality competition entries through creative writing workshops and one-to-one mentoring sessions. So I am particularly delighted to see, here, stories by some of the many promising writers I worked with alongside those pieces submitted independently to the competition. I know the judges found shortlisting the thirty entries that make up this collection difficult as there were many more that they would have liked to include.

The competition's theme was 'crossing the Tees' and entrants were encouraged to be inspired by that as long as their stories had a taste of the Tees Valley. You will, therefore, find this anthology packed with fantastic, diverse tales, everything from fantasy and historical fiction to crime and romance. But they all have one thing in common: they are brilliantly written creative reimaginings of a region rich in writing talent. So turn the pages and enjoy a magical armchair journey through Teesside.

Tracey Iceton
Author and Creative Writing Tutor
2018

WINNER

SLAGHEAP
MICHAEL JAMES PARKER

"And how are your sandwich-making skills?"

Andy almost laughs, thinking the youngin is joking until he realises he's not, and that his pinkish lips are pursed because he's deadly serious and not because he's suppressing a smirk at the question. Andy glances down to compose himself, spots the swell at the lad's chest, twigs the youngin is a lassie, so it's her being serious, and now the pinkish lips make more sense to him. Wonders if he's ballsed up. Takes too long, far too long, to answer the question. It's gotten away from him. Feels his ears redden, hears the steady thud of his blood surging to them. A bead of sweat draws down his right side, trundling over his ribcage. He squirms.

"Well, I've made them," he says. The laugh he forces is almost a wheeze.

She smirks at him. The peak of her black Subway cap casts shade across her eyes, which narrow as she next inhales, nostrils flaring so the flesh grows taut against the ring in each.

Fuck. Surely she can't smell it on him; wasn't even a quarter-bottle. And he's eaten since. He shifts in his seat and hears the paper-cellophane rustle of the Greggs bag in the inner pocket of his only suit, far too big on him now. Black: good for funerals and weddings and christenings and court appearances and job interviews.

"I think that's all. Have you got any questions for me, Andrew?"

He'd asked her to call him Andy.

He shakes his head, goes to stand, thinks of a question. He asks it from his strange new position, half-crouched, all angles, like something you'd expect to see scurrying in shadows out of the corner of your eye. The suit jacket sags away from his chest. He's making eye contact so doesn't see the exposed Greggs packet, but she does.

"Long do you think it will take to hear back?"

It's a sad smile on her face now, pitying. Lisa had worn that same smile when she'd told him she was taking the kids to her mam's down south for a week while he sorted himself out going on three years ago.

"Our manager will go through the CVs as quickly as he can. The aim is to let applicants know by the end of today, tomorrow at the latest."

Andy nods, rises, and leaves the Subway booth. Someone else, someone younger and fitter and, in Andy's eyes at least, far more employable, slips into the chair he's just vacated. He hears laughter of the kind he knows is aimed at him. He doesn't know how he knows it, it's the same way he knows up is up, the same node of self-preservation that gets him home when he's had a wild one. Suddenly, he's the Andy of old, four stone of smeltery-hardened muscle heavier, full of fuck with a roaring furnace at his core, and he's turned around, fists balled, before he swerves it, joining instead the end of the queue for Cooplands Bakeries with his head bowed, behind a youngin with rips in the arse of her jeans. He seethes there, shuffling forwards on the conveyor belt of potential employees.

He scans the room while he waits. Still the only one in a suit, though he's undecided on if that's a good or bad thing. Can't be any worse for his prospects than the rest of these, all t-shirts and jeans, most in trainers, some even in those daft beanie hats with words like 'Obey' and 'Destruct' on. Reckons he's the oldest there, or one of. A few faces he recognises from the JobCentre. None he ever bothers talking to. They're all junkies, smackheads who've never worked a day in their lives, not a thing like him. None of these have done a fourteen-hour shift hauling coke. None of these have baked in front of the blast furnace.

Some of them could be in the same boat though, built lives on broken promises like he did. The older ones, maybe; definitely not these students with their lives ahead of them and certainties to get these two-bob zero-hours contracts.

His mouth's dry, coated with a claggy film that seems

to cling to his tongue. Teeth feel like they've got jumpers on. Didn't he have a bottle of water? Must have left it somewhere. He coaxes some saliva under the tip of his tongue and swishes it around his mouth, skooshing it between his teeth. Lassie with the rips in her jeans turns and glares. He thought the noise was only in his head.

"Alright?" he asks.

She furnishes him with an infinitesimal smile, nothing more than a twitch of the facial muscle, and then her back's to him once more. She's next in line. The interviewer is wrapping things up, leaning forwards to shake the young lad's hand in the chair opposite, wishing him 'good luck'. It's as the interviewer stands that he spots Andy. His brow furrows, corrugated tin on an allotment shed.

"You've already seen me, mate," the interviewer says.

Andy looks behind him.

The rest of the queue gawks back.

Andy shakes his head.

The interviewer shuffles through a pile of CVs and brings out a grease-spotted one, yellower than the others, the paper creased where it's been in his pocket.

"Andrew Johnson," the interviewer reads.

That's him.

He has been here then. They're all the same. Cardboard fucking cut-out jobs. They'll go to these cardboard cut-out youngins. Roomful of divvies. The lassie in front barks a laugh, and now people at other booths turn to see what the commotion is. Jesus Christ, he's a man, not a fucking sideshow.

He leaves before he loses it, charging through the double-doors and out into the reception of Stockton Riverside College gym, cheap soles leaving black scuffs on the sports hall floor like shame. Follow to see a man with less than nowt. The receptionist jumps in her seat, opens her mouth, thinks better of it. There's a water cooler, and his hand trembles as he holds the plastic cup beneath the tap, water cold against his fingers. He necks three cups, clamps his molars against the sudden chill, slams the cup into the swing bin by the door, and pushes the bar.

Nothing.

He shoves the door.

Nothing.

"You've got to push the green button," says the receptionist.

"Should be a sign, then," Andy spits.

"There is," she says.

He slaps the green button.

The door hums open.

He stands in the car park with his hands on his head, squinting up into the mid-afternoon sun. His breath fogs. There are kids getting into and out of cars they've got no right to have at that age. They head into the jobs fair, their groups manoeuvring around him like a river's current around an obdurate boulder.

He stands there until he decides he's had enough, then leaves.

There are a few kids smoking on the edge of the car park, a yard or two from a sign proclaiming 'Stockton

Riverside College is a smoke free zone'. They move to let Andy pass.

"Now then, lads."

They smile awkwardly back at him.

"Couldn't lend a tab?"

Most of them mumble they don't have any spare, which he knows is a load of shite, but one lad digs a rollie out of a pack of Golden Virginia and hands it to him.

"Borrow a lighter?"

The same lad hands over a pink Clipper. Andy lights up, draws deeply, and hands the lighter back.

"Cheers."

The Infinity Bridge lurches from the water ahead. Not for the first time, he feels proud as he crosses. Those are his balustrades. His steel dampers stop the thing from shaking apart.

The letters on his grubby hall carpet fan out when he opens his front door. He snatches them up, shuffling past the two whose windows show red-tinted paper and bear Do Not Ignore stamps on the envelope. A plain brown one the JobCentre usually uses gets dropped onto the grime-coated kitchen table, disturbing a fine layer of dust. Stray strands of rolling tobacco fall to the peeling lino. Andy shots a pizza shop menu to one side and stops. In his hand he holds a postcard. The tremor is still there; the image of a row of Neapolitan ice cream-coloured beach houses is ablur with the severity of it.

For a moment, Andy doesn't want to turn it over. It's from the kids; nobody else would send him a postcard.

Clacton-on-Sea, the caption in the bottom-right of the picture says. No certainty that's where she's living with them, but it must be nearby, because he knows Lisa, and Lisa wouldn't take a long train journey with the three bairns, especially not now Ryan is three. Or will he be five? Then again, what if she hasn't gotten the train there at all? What if she's shacked up with a bloke who drives, and they just pile into his car and take trips and laugh at Andy?

He flips the postcard, rubbing the wedding band he still wears with his left thumb, as if wishing upon a magic lamp. The writing on the reverse is cramped and rushed, the joined-up characters difficult to read, exacerbated by the shaking of his hand. He shoves a pile of musty washing from the nearest chair and sits, oblivious to the pissy foist smell which wafts up in the washing's wake.

Head in hands, he reads.

"*Dad,*

Mam doesn't know I sent this. Tommy lent me the money for the stamp. I told him I wanted a can of pop. Tommy's working in a pub washing pots on the weekend for a fiver an hour. We're in Clacton for a break. It's probably colder in Middlesbrough. There are palm trees here but they don't have any leaves yet. Mam had to take us out of school for the week but they said it was cheaper paying the fine than it was to go in the holidays. I asked if we could come up and see you in the summer holidays but..."

Before he knows it the postcard is in tatters and he's done two bottles of White Lightning. Can't even remember what it said. He tries pushing the pieces back together like a jigsaw but he's got too thick a head to focus. There's a bit comes back to him, though: Tommy's got himself a job.

His fourteen-year-old son has got a job and he's not.

He's out the door, luckily still in his shoes. The wind picks up the end of his tie and flings it over his shoulder, and its icy fingers probe the gaps between his buttons in his shirtfront and the holes in the underarm of his suit jacket. He weaves through shoppers, past kids on their dinner hour, passes other men in better suits than his, men who give him a wide berth and peer down their noses at him.

What he remembers from the postcard propels him through the orange door of the amusements.

Glenn Miller plays over the speakers, accompanied by electronic jingles from the machines and drowned out by the occasional thunder of coins in returns chutes. He slips his card into the cashpoint and hits the button for three hundred.

Insufficient funds.

Checks his balance, supposed to be more than there is – fucking JobCentre, quick enough to take it back when they've overpaid but leave him waiting for what he's owed, probably so he has to go and beg for it – withdraws one-twenty.

He had a favourite, once, but it's been a while since and he can't spot it now. It's changed inside, but get past the paint job and the new carpet and it's still just pulsing lights, pensioners, pissheads.

The manager collars him three bad spins into roulette.

Andy wonders if he'd clocked him from the get-go and let him spunk his money before saying anything.

"Andy. You know you're barred."

Andy slurs something in response.

"Gerrup and piss off, lad."

The manager crosses his arms and puffs out his chest. A big lad lurks behind him. Andy unballs his fists, stuffs them into his swiftly-emptied pockets, and slinks out. Christ, he could do with a drink. There's a tenner left in the account and an offy not far from here hasn't barred him yet.

A phone rings. Andy jerks awake. It's dark now, the sky's a blossoming bruise of navy and purple, and he's cold to his marrow. The Infinity Bridge is stark as bone, the walkway a glowing red platform. He remembers fishing for salmon round here. Caught one once with a squealing Tommy.

Phone. He fumbles it out of his pocket. The Greggs bag is still there, sausage rolls smashed to crumbs.

"Hi, is this Mr Andrew Johnson?"

He unglues his tongue from the roof of his dry-as-desert mouth. He recognises the voice: the lassie from the Subway job.

"Aye. Yes, sorry."

"Mr Johnson, I'm really sorry, but unfort-"

He watches the phone tumble through the air, its lit screen blinking off as it plunges through the river's black surface. The ripples disturb the reflection of the bridge.

For the first time, he recognises the cruel irony in its name.

SECOND PLACE

A CROSSING
COLIN O' CAHAN

I watch from a respectable distance as my son and his new friends construct a small raft from twigs, twine and paper to cross the River Tees. His tongue just edging out on the left side of his mouth, just like his father. His dark curls sputter and roll in the English south-westerly wind. He is far too absorbed in his machinations to realise that I watch him from where I sit on the picnic blanket with the other mothers, but I do. The others enjoy their tea and sandwiches but I only play at enjoying myself. The woman who came from the council had said that it would be good for me to get out, so I'm out.

I watch as he deftly ties together two long sticks. His fingers are remarkably dexterous for a five year old. He laughs and smiles with his friends and the darkness that sits in my chest lifts for a moment. He seems happy. Is that not everything I could have hoped for? And yet, there remains a storm around me, blocking my view of land.

One of my new friends makes a joke and I laugh consciously. Yet still, I watch him. He holds up the little raft he has made and inspects it in the wan English sunlight. In truth it is nothing more than a few sticks. But he looks proud, and completely oblivious to the other meaning that raft holds, which is exactly how I want it to be. He waddles to the water's edge and it is all I can do not to rise and run after him. He will surely slip and fall. However, I know that the river at this point is merely a few feet deep. It is not the silent mass that stalks past the houses and loiters under the bridges of Middlesbrough.

Someone had told me recently of Peg Powler and how she would grab naughty children who ventured too close. I imagine her rising out of the water to greet him and catching his ankles, dragging him down the bank and into the viridian depths. I imagine his response would be to wave and attempt to show off his creation to the hag. He has lost all fear. He does not remember it.

I do. I remember another crossing only two years ago. The sky, I know, was this sky I see now, but it wasn't. It was terrible and black; it was an obsidian mirror for the sea, reflecting nothing but my fears. The sea, we were told, was the safest way. I did not know exactly where we were going, but I knew I did not want him to have to remember the way we got there. I held him to me the whole way. I do not honestly believe he experienced that crossing as anything other than being close to my breast.

He lays his little handicraft in the river and it floats lazily away. He squeals for joy and races after it. The water, even here, is too strong and it pulls away from him, sending the raft darting off into the distance. He looks at me and for a moment I think he is about to cry, for a fraction of a second I think he remembers.

The sea destroyed us. It beat us mercilessly from all sides. In the pitch black, with only a clouded moon to guide us, I remember never knowing where the waves were coming from until they hit. I remember squeals of fright, sharp intakes of breath and terrible silences. I wish to remember nothing of the one woman I saw thrown from her seat and who I never saw again.

He totters up to me, his crossing unsuccessful this time around. He smiles lazily, squinting at me. He asks for a sandwich, burbling still in a mix of English and Arabic, although with a hint of a northern accent that I cannot decide if I love or loathe. He seems content enough today playing with his friends. I appreciate the little things, like the fact he seems to have no fear of the water. Or perhaps the river here with its lazy flow and verdant banks is so far removed from the salt spray and terror of our crossing that the two do not even register as one.

The darkness was terrifying, but the light brought its own horrors. I saw a bloated corpse floating next to our dingy. The woman's dark clothing macabrely transformed into a deathly life jacket. She was not the same woman I had seen thrown from her seat. She may not have even been from our boat. The fact was it was becoming hard to separate the faces I saw. All of them merged until my only true point of reference was my son. I had to keep looking at him just to remind myself of who I was. To stop myself becoming one with the mass of bodies. To retain an identity beyond that of an immigrant.

That same fear still lingers now. When I am out shopping or walking with my son to school, I worry that people will see me as an intruder, as an unwanted presence in their lives. I worry that I will mispronounce some word or that I will forget to perform one of the litany of English niceties and be revealed for what I am. One of the swarm that entered uninvited, without knocking, without wiping our feet, without politely declining any offer of hospitality. I worry that I sound angry or ungrateful. I worry that I am angry.

One of the other mothers is telling a story about how she used to spend her weekends here as a child. I know we are just outside of the city but the sounds and the smells are of another world. The grass here has a different quality to any grass I have ever experienced back home. It is softer and grows closer together, becoming more like a carpet than a plant. The greens too are deeper, more pronounced. There is not the same welcoming haze of heat hanging in the air. But there is a quality even more intangible than that. A feeling that truly separates here from home. Although I am still not used to it, there is an implicit safety here. The only planes that fly are delivering people. The only sounds of warfare are child's play.

Home was no place for a child. I told my husband

this often, although I did not seriously think we would leave. I thought at most we would go to my parents in the countryside and wait out the worst of it. But it spread, and did not stop, until every city and town in my home was infected. I do not remember the exact moment, but the realisation came that this was not a disease we were going to beat. We gathered all of our savings – now gone – and packed what we could carry. Then we left. My son and I. His father was killed two days before. There are times when I cannot bear to look at my son because he has his face and I cannot stand the constant reminder of what was taken from me.

This is not one of those times. He is smiling. He wanders slowly back to the river's edge and gazes across. He is too small to wade across the river, but perhaps when he is older he will be able to cross. Perhaps he will be able to when he is bigger, when it is safe. For now, he is happy here I tell myself, unsure if I am. He is safe here.

THIRD PLACE

BEYOND THE BRIDGE
ETHEL STIRMAN

She stands alone under the bridge. Hardly more than twenty years of age, she could have been beautiful but everything about her is overdone, as if she is trying too hard. Her clothes are bright but cheap, straight from Primani: top low cut, skirt too tight, shoes too high. Long dark hair, pulled tightly back into a luxurious ponytail, frames a painted doll face.

Nervously glancing this way and that, she is obviously waiting for someone to appear. Stepping up to the edge of the kerb, she smiles as a car approaches, lights blinding her momentarily but it speeds past oblivious to her charms.

Retreating to her station beside the wall, she leans wearily against it, retrieves a cigarette from her shoulder bag, lights it, drawing the noxious fumes deep into her lungs, blowing out smoke rings which rise high into the cold night air before dispersing to nothing. Anything to dispel the boredom or is it to keep her mind from the danger of her position?

This is definitely not a nice area. The walls behind her are grimed and run with damp. Mould and grotesque mushrooms inhabit its crevices. The pavement beneath her feet is cracked and broken. In dark corners the stench of urine is overpowering. Few venture here. Cars pass infrequently on their way to cross the Tees to escape from this rundown part of the city. The only other sound comes from the Transporter Bridge as it grinds and rattles its way across the river with monotonous regularity.

Further down the road, a car draws up and dims its bright lights. The young woman takes a mobile from her bag and speaks surreptitiously into it, bending to adjust her sandal strap, before replacing it in her bag. The passenger door opens and what seems to be a young girl alights from the car and starts walking towards her. The car zooms away, tyres screeching in its haste to be away from the scene.

The girl is engrossed in counting the money she holds in her hand, peeling off some notes and secreting them in her bra. Looking up, she suddenly realises she is not alone. Stuffing the rest of the cash into her pocket, she approaches her warily.

"Who are you? This is my patch. You'd better scarper quick before Johnnie turns up and catches you at it!"

"Sorry, I didn't realise. I'm a bit new to all this. My name's Sindy," she says, stretching out her hand which was promptly ignored by the other girl who looks her up and down warily.

"My name's Charlotte," she replies, "but most people call me Charlie."

Charlie looks as if she might be about twenty-five but is trying to look much younger. Her baby blonde hair obviously comes from a bottle and is curled so that it cascades over her left shoulder. Wide blue eyes shine unnaturally in the dim light and appear over-large, enhanced by false, black eyelashes. She is dressed in a similar way to Sindy: short skirt, plunging top, except she has a fake fur jacket draped over her shoulders.

"You got anyone to look out for you?"

Sindy casts her eyes downwards and shakes her head. "My old man threw me out, when he finally got tired of using me as a punchbag." She registers the sympathy in the other girl's eyes.

"Guess you'd better hang around here with me 'til Johnnie comes. He's not a bad guy as 'friends' go."

"Is Johnnie your pimp, then?"

Charlie laughs softly. "Don't ever let him hear you calling him that, he don't like it. He thinks he's doing us girls a friendly favour – sort of if you scratch my back, I won't scratch yours kinda arrangement. Bit like a modern Fagin, I suppose."

"Maybe I should just go," Sindy suggests but Charlie will have none of it.

"You don't want to do that, love." She looks around as if checking they can't be overheard. "Haven't you heard? There's someone after us 'ladies'. Another girl disappeared last night."

"All the more reason to clear off. Has anyone reported it to the filth?"

"You gotta be jokin'. What they gonna do? They don't care if one of us goes missing. A few less will make their job easier, I reckon. Although there's one or two of them might miss their 'favourites' if you get my meaning. No, Johnnie and the other lads will see us alright."

Charlie walks forward and puts a protective arm around Sindy's shoulders. Johnnie will be pleased to have a new girl to replace the hapless Monica. "Don't worry, you'll be safe with me and I'll be glad of a bit of company. It gets lonely under this old bridge but not for long if we're lucky."

It isn't long before a car pulls up down the road and flashes its lights three times.

"I'll have to go," Charlie explains, "one of my regulars." She runs quickly towards the car, a plastic smile plastered on her lips.

Sindy shivers. What are these girls thinking, putting themselves at risk? She hopes Charlie will be safe. It is time to get out of here. She certainly does not want to be around when Johnnie turns up. Walking past the end of the bridge, she turns towards the van parked just around the corner. Lights flash in recognition and she opens the passenger side door and climbs in quickly.

Kicking off her shoes, she turns to the driver. "Turn the heater up, Tony, it's perishing out there."

Tony adjusts the heater controls to maximum. "Did you get anything, Sarah? I wish you'd wear a wire so we can listen in and know exactly what's going on. It would be much safer."

"Not if I get caught wearing one, it won't. Don't worry, you'll hear me if anything goes wrong. I'm not stupid enough to actually get into a car, you know."

Tony knows there is nothing more to be said on the subject. He might not like it, but Sarah is his senior so there isn't anything he can do about it.

Pulling on a police overcoat, Sarah stretches out her long legs and makes herself comfortable. "Let's get back to the station so I can put in my report. It'll be nice to get to bed before midnight for once."

Further down the street, deep in the shadows, a figure watches them as they drive away. A match flares as he lights a cigarette before stepping out into the light of the street lamp. He crosses the road, unlocks the middle car of three parked there, gets in and drives off in the opposite direction to the van.

The following night Sarah, as Sindy, takes up her position under the bridge. It is raining outside, making the night even more miserable. She waits. A car pulls up beside her and the passenger window is lowered. She stoops so that she can see the occupant of the car. Her heart is racing. What if it is someone she knows? This thought always haunts her.

"How much?" growls the punter.

"Sorry, love, I'm waiting for one of my regulars. Maybe tomorrow, huh?"

It is her standard response now. They never bother arguing; after all, there are plenty more girls like her on the streets.

"You're new around here, aren't you?" the punter asks. "I've never seen you before."

"Yeah," Sarah replies, smiling ruefully. "Used to work over Stockton but I had a bit of bother with one of the other girls. She won."

"You seen Charlie tonight? She's usually around about this time."

"Naw, not seen her at all. She must be 'busy'." Sarah looks puzzled. Come to think of it, where is Charlie? She should be here by now.

Suddenly another car pulls in behind the first one, a black Audi with smoked windows. Sarah's heart takes a leap as the driver gets out and comes round the car towards her. She wants to run but stands her ground. The man could have stepped straight out of an eighties movie, tall and tanned, with gelled black hair and gleaming white veneers. She can feel his eyes through the dark glasses he wears but holds her nerve and waits for him to make the first move.

"You Sindy?" His voice is as smooth and silky as his appearance.

She nods silently.

"Charlie told me about you. You seen her?"

This must be Johnnie, Sarah thinks. "No, she hasn't

been round here. You don't think something's happened to her, do you?" She doesn't have to fake concern, she really is worried for the girl who showed her nothing but kindness the previous night.

"She didn't show up this afternoon and she's not answering her mobile. None of the other girls have seen her and it's not like her to drop out of sight." He is trying to keep the concern out of his voice. Maybe he is as much a friend as a minder, after all. "Here's my card. Ring if you hear anything at all, okay? It might be best if you go home for the night. It's getting too dangerous for you to be out on the streets alone. Come to see me tomorrow and we'll sort out an arrangement."

Sarah wishes he would take off those glasses so that she can see his eyes. You can tell so much more from a person's eyes. Not trusting her voice, she simply nods her agreement.

He pauses before getting into his car. "Can I give you a lift somewhere?"

"No, it's alright. I don't live far."

Once he is out of sight, Sarah leaves the shelter and makes her way to the unmarked police car that is parked opposite the bridge tonight. Tony is surprised at her early return.

"I need you to put out an all-points bulletin on a missing girl."

He raises his eyebrows in response. She gives a detailed description of Charlie over the radio. It may already be too late.

The figure once again regards them from his vantage point in the darkened doorway opposite. As they drive away, he climbs into a blue Range Rover. This time, however, he follows them instead of heading in the opposite direction. He maintains his distance. He has no fear of losing them, he knows where they are going.

Back at the station, Sarah dives into a hot shower, eager to strip Sindy from her skin. Although, at first, she had been flattered when the DI had suggested she went under cover, she had not expected to identify so much with her role. She and Sindy might stand on polar ends of society but they were both dependent on more powerful men to survive. Now she feels a great deal of empathy for these girls who often have few choices beyond their profession. Most arrive there out of desperation.

All eyes turn on her as she enters the main office. A dozen or so officers sit around waiting for her debriefing. She quickly appraises them of the facts and gives them a detailed description of Charlie, the latest girl to go missing: five four, bleached hair, cheap clothes, skinny, track marks. It is not a pretty picture.

"Her pimp hasn't seen her since twelve last night when she dropped off her takings," she continues. "The other victims have all been found on rough, open ground but quite close to footpaths. It's almost as if he wants us to find the bodies quickly."

The officers mutter amongst themselves as they make notes on their pads. Every one of them is eager to find the murderer. There could be a promotion in it.

Sarah designates duties. Three officers to go to the girl's flat and make follow-up enquiries amongst the neighbours. Two more to work the riverside area; someone may have seen something. A couple of detectives to contact whatever informants they thought might be useful. Perhaps they should bring Johnnie in for questioning. Time is of the essence.

The call comes in at ten o'clock the next morning. A body has been found on the waste ground beside the river. It is a young woman matching the missing girl's description. She was found naked, like the others arranged in a foetal position, ten yards from the footpath. Although it is hard to be sure, there is no apparent evidence of sexual violence.

Sarah feels the life drain from her. She has not slept in twenty four hours. Only the faint hope of finding Charlie has kept her going. Now she can go home to bed and leave the detective work to her colleagues for a few hours. Sindy will be back on the streets tonight.

As she is leaving, DI Tom Princeton calls her over. "Give me a minute, Sarah, and I'll run you home. You must be bushed." He throws her his car keys. "Why don't you wait for me in the car?"

It's times like these that catch her unawares. She's never particularly cared for her boss; his broad smile and kindly eyes always seem a bit forced to her. "I won't say no, boss," she replies. "I'm just about done in."

Crossing the parking lot, she can't help feeling there is something she is missing. Some link that is niggling at the back of her mind. She is so tired. She pulls herself into the passenger seat of the four by four, the leather seats cradling her weary body. She starts as Tom opens the driver's door and climbs in beside her.

"Right, young lady, let's get you home. You live over the river, don't you? Your mum will be worried about you."

Sarah smiles; it's a long time since she lived at home. "No sir, I have one of the flats on The Green. My parents live in Leicester."

They are approaching the Transporter Bridge. It stands like a sentinel, straddling the Tees, guarding it against unwanted aliens, a filigree of blue girders reflecting the strength and durability of the area's industrial past.

Luckily, it is running today. They join the short queue of cars waiting to cross the river. Sarah can feel herself drifting into sleep but is forced awake by the clanging and grinding as the bridge docks. The gates swing open and cars and pedestrians spew forth heading into Middlesbrough.

Tom starts the engine. She is slipping away again lulled by the steady thrum of the Range Rover. There is a slight jolt as they board but Sarah remains oblivious.

Progressing gently over the river, Tom ponders on the changes he has seen. Once the waters were almost eclipsed by vessels from all over the globe. Sights and sounds of a throbbing industrial port had filled the air. Now the river moved gracefully towards the sea, a blue ribbon sparkling in the winter sunshine. The docks almost antiseptic in their cleanliness. He has always admired this, the first bridge, innovative in its day, now protected as an historical monument, a relic of the past, just like him. It is time to go.

He smiles as he watches the slip of a girl beside him. What right has she to think she could follow in his footsteps? Women don't belong on his Force. He laughs softly. She has been much more convincing as Sindy than Sarah. He doesn't like women much, especially not pushy women who think they can wrap men around their little finger.

Docking at the landing stage at Port Clarence, Sarah sleeps on as they make their way past industrial premises that line the roads. This had been his first beat. The blue Range Rover pulls off the road onto the waste ground behind The Station Hotel. Sarah stirs as the vehicle draws to a halt.

Stretching her arms high, she pauses with them still in mid-air as she suddenly realises where they are. Eyes wide, she turns questioningly to the man beside her.

"Why are we here, sir?" but Tom Princeton offers no explanation. His eyes bright, a sickly sneer twists his face as he reaches out, encircles her neck with his hands, subjugates her with his manliness.

Someone walking a familiar path, will find her lifeless body, returned to the innocent it once was.

HIGHLY COMMENDED

SOMETIMES THE GODS COLLUDE WITH US
MARIANNE AMY

We're hanging about on the bridge in Yarm, leaning on the old stone wall. I take a newspaper cutting from my purse.

"Here's the advert, Sal." I poke it towards her.

She half turns and lights a ciggy.

"THIS SUNDAY. THE JIMMIE HENDRIX EXPERIENCE - No.25 in the charts. Jimmy is the rave of the London scene..." I read. "They've spelt his name wrong in two different ways. It's J.I.M.I."

Sal yawns. Her breath is steaming up the January night.

"You're not fussed, are you?" I keep pushing. "Our Tommy says he's gonna be a big star, seen him in London. The Beatles were in the audience!"

"I am fussed!" Sal's lying. "I feel the same about Mean Dean! You're not fussed about him though, are ya?"

"That's different, you berk!"

I've had an eyeful of Sal and this fella she's meeting tonight. She's had an eyeful of me and Jimi.

"7/6, it says here. We won't have to pay that."

Sal changes the subject and flicks a glance of approval over my dress. "Your mam make that?"

She's looking a little envious.

"Yep. One of her customers had an extra ream, let her keep it to say thank you. Canny, in't it?"

A motor roars up the bridge, beeping as it passes us, slowing down.

"It's Lenny!"

"About bloody time!"

We rush over best we can in our nippy slingbacks, me teetering along with a ciggy and a bulging carpet bag and Sal running in front on her toes, pumping her goosey young Cilla legs. A burgundy Vitesse stops at the side of the road and Sal helps herself into the back. I follow.

"Hiya Lenny! Ace new wheels!"

"Come in front."

"I'll sit next to Sal. I wanna…'

"In the front," he barks.

I hesitate. Who's he think he is, me dad? But Lenny's not someone you say no to.

"I've got something for you in a bit," he proffers.

So I do as he says.

I settle onto the grooved, ice-cold leather, cringing as his pale eyes run up my thighs. He can't help himself when I'm in my dead short dresses. Perv. He's known me since I was in nappies. Sal ribs me about him, saying I should "put Big Lenny out of his misery", whatever that means. A butcher and a boxer, he's a friend of my older brother, Tommy, who asked Lenny to look after me at The Kirk when he's not there himself.

The windows mist up against the baltic road, wheeling around farmland to the club. Half way there, Lenny's fist passes over my right knee and hovers without touching it. I open my hand beneath it as he dispenses four blue pills.

"Ah, ta, Lenny!"

I pass two to Sal in the back. She's opening the silver hip flask I've nicked from dad, containing the gin I've nicked from mam. She swipes the pills.

"Down the hatch! Here's to a good un! You want a slug, Len?"

I know he won't.

"I've swallowed mine." He always does that, takes pills with no drink.

"Two of 'em?" Sal pulls a face.

"Aye, about that. Straight no chaser." He tosses a box of cigs onto my lap. "Take 'em in with ya."

I turn the scarlet box over. "Thanks Len... Craven A? Our Granny Wheeler smokes them! You 'ad a special delivery, Buffalo Len?"

Sal laughs explosively through gin-pursed lips, which starts me off too. I feel a bit nervous though. 'Buffalo Len' is his boxing name and he hates it taken in vain.

Lenny just keeps driving.

We bank into the Kirk's car park, triggering a Pavlovian response – butterflies. Swinging my legs out the car, my lilac patents crush a patch of ground frost, sparkling and setting.

Light-hearted and tingly, I tip my face up to the indigo canopy. Chinks of crystal wink at me, as I silently ask for more excitement.

Big Lenny shrugs into his bouncer's overcoat as we amble to the front of the club. Me and Sal are getting chatty. The pills are befriending our blood. Lenny stops to discuss something with John, his boss. He's seen me loads of times but rarely acknowledges me.

Maybe he knows I'm only fifteen and turns a blind eye.

I'm eager to get in, have a cig and a beer. Sal, shamelessly on heat, is looking around for that bloke.

"I swear you're sniffin' the air for him, Sal!"

She wallops me pretty hard on the bum.

Lenny has to see us through the door if we want free entry. Tapping my foot, the men gab on while Sal sniffs the floor for suitable pheramones. I fix my eyes on the Esso sign near the side of the building. Beneath the sign, a huddle of musicians stalk towards the artists' entrance, leaving an old Ford Thames parked haphazardly near the petrol pump. Three of them walk close together – two white men and one striking coloured man – all laughing at something. This trio look strangely alike. It has to be the Jimi Hendrix Experience. All of them with wild hair and smart jackets with embroidery. I can see Jimi Hendrix – it has to be him – long-legged, dead slim and like some kind of spaceman. Ruffles around his neck, Chelsea boots with a Cuban heel and his guitar closely slung around his back, reminding me of a baby in a papoose. Behind the trio, one man's carrying a lot of equipment, he's pretty bogged down. Another man, really tall and well built, in a suit and mop-top haircut, walks ahead of them as if scouting for something.

Lenny stops chatting and looks behind him to see what's making me smile. I'm yanking Sal's coat sleeve, focusing on the tallest man over there. "In't that tall mop-top one from The Animals?"

"Yep!"

John suddenly notices me. Maybe I look eighteen tonight. "Ex-bassist – Chas Chandler! Good friend of mine – managing the band – got Jimi over from America. You getting a lift home with Lenny? You can meet 'em after!" he says.

He shoots off towards the band. A fairy godmother just stole John's body to grant me a wish I'd never even asked.

"D'ya hear that, Sal?"

She nods and grins. Lenny looks at his polished boots. I see him clench his jaw and fists, ever so briefly.

Anticipation fuses with smoke near the stage, where all the muso's gather. Wafts of reefer get stronger as I edge my way to the front. The Experience are setting up – tuning, turning dials, chiming notes, tapping cymbals – wizards preparing a ritual. Jimi Hendrix glides onstage and tunes his guitar in seconds, fiddling with his feet on pedals and wotnot. My palms bristle. He looks serious and his hair's teased right out, so the meagre stage lights bless him with a fuzzy halo. He seems too big for the room and I could grab the ankle of his fancy trousers if I want. I nearly do, just for a laugh. He looks down at me, right in my eyes, then smiles like a little boy. Has he heard my thoughts?

I go to smile back but I can't, I'm staring agog till he turns back to his guitar. Dying to tell Sal, but she's off with Prince Charming somewhere and I'm partly glad, because he wouldn't notice me if she was here, flaunting her brooding Mediterranean eyes and long legs.

It's taking a bit for the small crowd to adjust to Jimi. They're an R&B bunch and loads of them are booing at 'Wild Thing', but I'm spellbound. Everything about him is magic. He's bending down on both knees, right in front of me – lurching back on himself, till his head's on the floor, coming back up, playing behind his back and the crowd are finally getting into it. I'm convinced he's come down from the stars. Lights have come on in my mind. I know who I want to be, I know what I want to do. I know what kind of fella I'd love and I know what kind of dress I'm asking our mam to make next. The music's getting louder and he's playing increasingly far out stuff – blowing the lid off this little Teesside joint – and doing things with his guitar that make me blush.

The thought of meeting him after is making me giddy. I sip on some ale to bring me back to earth.

Lenny's at the front of the stage, off to the side. He's facing the punters, but keeps looking up at Jimi, then slyly looking over at me. I don't let on I've seen.

I'm waiting at the stage for Sal. She pounces on me from the side and grabs my shoulder.

"Alright?" Sal's looking sheepish. Something's up.

"Did you see him?" I ask excitedly, pretending I've not cottoned on. I'm not making this easy for her.

"Course I did! Where d'you think I've been? He's got these gorgeous lips and he's…"

I roll my eyes. "I meant flamin' Jimi Hendrix! I bet you never even looked, did you?"

"Well, I heard him." She looks at me with plaintive Betty Boop eyes. "Mel, I'm gonna split the scene with Dean." She performs a daft jive with the rhyme, but I'm not laughing.

"Him and his mates are hitch…"

"You what?" I laugh in disbelief. "You're gonna hitchhike instead of a lift back and meeting the band?"

Sal's stood chewing her bottom lip.

"How will I stay at yours now? You're not going back home are you?"

"He's having a little party! I'll give you the address, you can come with Lenny. I'll get the addr…"

"Sal! Why can't you just come with me and stop being a drag? His nob's not gonna fall off before next weekend, is it!"

"I know, but I feel sick Mel, I need some fresh air… and some lovin'!"

"You need ya head read, that's what you need!" I'm resigning myself to unknown fate.

"Mel, come with us!" She doesn't mean it. "You're me best mate!" Rubbing my hand, hers are very clammy. She's chewing like a moron.

"Give over, Sal! You've got yourself rabid! 'Ow many pills you had now? Has he bin givin' you drugs?"

"No! He doesn't do uppers, he just smokes a bit of reefer and drinks ale. I've not had more than you!"

I let her go. She's always putting lads before mates. I can stay at Lenny's if I really have to. I know that and so does she.

Lenny won't give me more pills. Sal gone, house lights on and the soulless sound of broken glass being swept, men shouting over one another, a spell is broken. A handful of us move upstairs to a pretty grotty back room. Both bands of the night are in there with others milling about. I'm the only girl and I feel well out of it. John comes over with Chas Chandler and hands me a warm bottle of Newkie Brown.

"Right!" he begins. "Chas, this is, ah…"

My stomach leaps. "Mel," I say, trying not to goof.

"Chas – Mel – friend of Big Lenny over there." He jerks his head towards Lenny and 'Little Dave', another bouncer, messing about with Jimi doing arm-wrestling. What is Lenny playing at?

Chas holds his hand out to me, friendly enough but I wouldn't mess. I go to shake it but he takes my hand and gives it a quick kiss. John is already out the door.

"I'll be back," Chas says, "I've to sort the fees oot with Johnny."

I'm looking askance at Jimi. He's won the wrestle. He's making his way over to Chas and me, but Chas leaves before he sees. Jimi keeps coming towards me, smiling. I look behind to see if someone else is on his radar.

"Hey," he speaks softly in his American tone. 'Didn't I see you at the stage before? You're beautiful, you're like an angel."

"Yeah," I say shakily, smiling awkwardly. The pills've made my mouth dry. I take a clumsy swig of ale and cover up a drip down my chin, not that he's looking at my chin.

He's looking in my eyes. My high's picking up again. I feel warm. I'm wobbly-kneed like a screen heroine.

"Thanks... uh... I loved the show... I mean I really did, I'm not just saying it."

Jimi laughs modestly, then Lenny comes barging in.

"I've got another one for you. 'Walk the Bottle'." He's looking at me.

Bloody Lenny. I sit on a beer crate as Jimi turns politely away to join him and Little Dave. I'm bummed out, but Chas comes back in and sits next to me on another crate, he's watching the game intently and drinking fast. We've not even started a conversation when Jimi wins the game. You'd think Lenny'd know when to give up, but he's had too many pills, like Sal. Knocking back Newkie as well.

"The nigger wins again!"

I watch his daft gob form the words and spit them out like arrows, just as Jimi comes back towards me and Chas.

Chas flies off the crate and barrels into Lenny, quick as a flash.

Thwack! It's the sickening slam of a hard fist hitting a soft cheek. It's in slow motion.

Lenny's face swings to the side and I swear I can see each bit of saliva flying out his mouth as he loses consciousness. He falls like a stuntman, back over the banister, a rock dislodged from a mountain. Thwock! is the dull smack of his bulk on the dancefloor below us – dead buffalo.

The loudest voice I've ever heard bellows, "Everybody out!"

It's John, trying to stop a fight before Little Dave gets his big head round the matter.

People scatter. Jimi turns to me, beckoning to come with them. I shake my head. He beckons more urgently – laughing – that sunny face. I shake my head. He briefly holds his heart with both hands, like a broken Romeo. Chas pushes him toward the staircase at the far end of the room and Jimi waves, turning his back. John grabs my elbow, steering me to the same staircase but I rive myself free and run the opposite way to get to Lenny.

Lenny's laid out, his right eye already a puce balloon.

"Oh, Len. You daft sod!" I mutter, as I crouch alone

with him on the vacant dance floor, awash with arcs from the mop.

All those happy footprints gone, for now.

John comes bustling through, carrying a jacket over his forearm with a tender kind of reverence. "Could you hold this a minute?" he asks a bit bossily, looking down at Lenny.

"It's Jimi's jacket – ripped on a beer crate! I'm getting it fixed."

"My mam's a seamstress!" I offer, delighted. "She'll do it for ya!"

"Fab!" says John, frowning at Lenny as though he is a smashed bottle of plonk on a packed night. "Take it and give me a price later – trust you won't lose it – give it to Lenny when it's done – if he makes it. Or bring it here next time you come."

He's off again, leaving me with Big Buffalo Lenny, stirring but not ready to move. I check Jimi's jacket over, ripped on the right arm and elbow. I feel the soft, maroon velvet and gold silk lining. Lifting it surreptitiously to my face, I breathe. I can smell his story – the DNA in his sweat – and just a hint of posh cologne.

•

With special thanks to John McCoy and Stan Laundon.

HIGHLY COMMENDED

OF GODS AND GOATS
ANN CUTHBERT

'Among the finds [in the River Tees] were a hairpin and a small lead goat.'
Time Team investigation, Piercebridge, 2009.

The goat had gone again. Chewed through its tether and made off.

"By Mercury!" he swore. That creature could move as fast as the god himself. He stood for a few moments, staring at the length of rope dangling from the iron hoop nailed to the shed, twisted it a couple of times as if to make sure the goat hadn't just turned invisible, then looked around. Where had it got to this time?

The sun wasn't up yet and there was a chill to the air that said winter wasn't far away. Thin mist hovered above the grass where dew hung but at least the rain had stopped. All around, he could hear the sounds of the camp stirring, men's shouts, the rattling of pans as they prepared breakfast. One group was setting off today to repair the road further north and already they were getting their gear together.

Where was that blasted goat? Felix, they called it. Lucky. Soon, his comrades would be arriving to give it a pat, rub off some of its luck to guard them against the dangers they'd face out in the countryside. No luck for him, though. It had to go and disappear on his watch.

He scouted round the barrack block closest to where he'd tethered the animal. No obvious tracks. It would take him hours to search all potential hideouts. That goat could squeeze into the narrowest spaces, climb up onto low sheds, overhanging roofs even, or just keep going until it found something – anything – to eat.

Another noise pushed its way into his head. A rushing, roaring noise. The river! Swollen by the recent rain and the water coming down off the hills, it had turned in the last few days into a spinning, foaming torrent. Surely the blasted creature hadn't gone down there?

He set off at a run, swerved between buildings, almost fell when he wobbled into a gutter. Someone shouted to him from the smithy, "What's up, Dannicus? Centurion ask you to do some work?" but he didn't break stride to retort.

He clambered up the wooden steps at the side of the gate-tower, praying that the guard wouldn't spot him. At the top, he leaned over the parapet and caught his breath before straightening and looking out at the river. The swirling water mesmerised him. Could goats swim? He wasn't sure but even the strongest soldier would have a hard time in that. Well, there was no sign of Felix down there. Nothing else for it. He would just have to brazen it out, pretend the goat was sick, that he'd bedded it down with some sweet hay and was keeping it out of everyone's way until it recovered. No one would want to pat a sick goat, even a lucky one...

Something had woken her. The beasts were shifting in their stalls, creaking the willow hurdles with their heavy bodies. There was another sound too, a rhythmic beat which carried in the early morning stillness. She knew it was made by feet, tramping along the straight new road the Strangers had laid over the old trackway. Dozens of feet, human and animal, because there were carts too. She could hear them trundling over the stones, heading north. Romans, they called themselves. Everyone was a Roman now, so they said. She snorted. If she hadn't been in bed, she would have spat.

She pulled the blanket up and tried to sleep again. But the other sound was back now, the voices that would not let her be. The Mothers, bidding her visit them in their shrine on the island.

"Come, Vatta, come!" they called.

It was a relief when she heard someone moving around, stirring the smouldering embers, lifting more logs onto the hearth. She heard the rattle of a spoon against a bowl then more voices, physical ones this time, as her family came towards the fire to break their fast.

"Tes water's living up to her name," she heard her eldest son say.

She knew what he meant. She'd heard that sound too, the boiling, surging river that ran close to their house. The soldiers had crossed it this morning on their way north. Easy for them now they'd built that new bridge.

"Our side of the walkway's been totally swept away." The voice was that of her youngest granddaughter, who would give birth to her first child very soon. Another reason why she must visit the Mothers. She curled her legs up beneath the blanket then straightened them to ease her joints. She'd thought she might manage to hobble to the walkway but, if it was gone as Brina said, how would she to get to the island now? She needed to get to there, to stop those voices, to find out what they wanted.

"Come, Vatta, come."

She pulled the blanket over her head, clapped her hands to her ears but it was no good. She couldn't block them out...

Sweating and tired, the men packed away the training gear, the heavy wooden swords and javelins and the wickerwork shields. Thank Mercury there'd been no route march today. He'd have a bit of time now to look for Felix before it got dark. He hadn't dared to search during work time although he had sneaked out to the shed twice just in case, by some good fortune, it had come back.

In the barrack room, he excused himself from cooking. "Not hungry tonight," he told them.

"What? Eat-all-you-can Dan's not hungry? Must be in love, eh, lads?"

"Guilty conscience more like. What tricks you up to now?"

He held his stomach. "Bad guts. Must've caught it off the goat," and he shut the door on their laughter.

Outside, he headed for the shed and got the cart. He had a hunch Felix might have crossed the bridge. There was plenty of good browsing over that side. Worth a look, he thought.

"Off to the settlement to get some hay for the goat," he said and trundled his cart out quickly before the gatekeeper could ask any questions. At the entrance to the bridge, he found the evidence he needed, a small pile of droppings. Walking across, he looked down at the river which foamed and bubbled beneath him, splashing high against the stanchions. Waves washed onto the sacred island in the middle. He could see that the walkway from the settlement side had been swept away although on the camp side it was still intact, for now. He felt in the purse at his belt, took out a small coin and dropped it into the water. Maybe the spirit of the river would help him find Felix.

The sun was going down now and the round houses of the settlement were silhouetted against a pink-streaked sky. Behind them stood a small hill, covered in prickly-looking bushes. It would certainly make a good hiding place for a runaway goat. At the door of one of the houses, sitting on a low stool with a blanket wrapped around her shoulders, was an old woman. He was aware of her eyes on him as he walked up the road. As he passed, she cleared her throat, hawking up a gob of spittle which just missed his boots.

He reached the hillock and stood looking up at it then took his knife from his belt and began to climb. Thorns snagged his cloak and scratched his arms as he tried to hack his way through the bushes. He put a hand to his face and brought away a smear of blood. He cursed himself for not bringing an axe.

"Blasted goat!" he shouted, as he turned back down the road and took hold of the handles of the cart. Behind him, he thought he heard a jeering bleat.

The old woman had her head down now but he knew she was still watching him. She'd probably be gathering up phlegm ready for a second attack. Just before he got into the firing line, he called to her, more a joke than a real question.

"Evening, Granny. Have you seen a goat?"

Her head jerked up and she looked straight at him…

She hadn't expected this. He was from the Strangers' camp but she could understand him. He spoke her language or at least a version of it. And, as it happened, she had seen a goat, a very handsome he-goat with curved horns and a thick brown-spotted fleece. It had trotted past her earlier in the day then chomped its way into the grove of thorn bushes on the hillock, the same one this silly boy had been trying to push his way into.

"Maybe I have," she said. "Why do you ask?"

"It's my goat," he said. "Well, not mine really. It belongs to the cohort and I was looking after it and then it escaped and it's a good-luck charm and if I don't get it back, my life won't be worth living."

He looked so miserable that she felt herself relenting. She could help him get it back. Anyway, she thought, one good turn deserves another. He could help her get to the island.

She took hold of her stick and held out her other hand to him.

"Help me up."

He leaned down and put his arm under her armpit. She grasped his shoulder and heaved herself upright. Still holding her by the arm, he supported her as she hobbled towards the hill.

"Let go now," she said and, with the aid of her stick, took her own weight. Head down, she crooned for a few moments then straightened herself and began a high-pitched ululation which took him by surprise. How could such a powerful sound come from such a frail body?

Nothing happened. Well, what had he expected, really? The goat had done for him this time.

Then, he saw bushes quivering, glimpsed horns, a head grinning at him. Soon, the whole goat emerged and trotted down the hill towards the old woman, stopping stock-still in front of her. While she bent to pat it, he reached inside his cloak and untied the rope from round his waist. When he looped it over the goat's head, it tugged away but, at a word from the woman, it settled and looked up at him with those odd, sideways eyes.

"Blasted goat!" he said, but he was smiling now. "Thank you, Granny."

But he didn't smile for long. He really didn't know how to smuggle the goat back into the camp. He'd had the vague plan of getting it into the cart and covering it over but now he realised how foolish the idea was. This goat wouldn't come quietly.

The old woman seemed to know what he was thinking. She bent over again and whispered in Felix's ear. The creature's eyes closed, its body went slack and it did not resist when he heaved it, muscles straining, into the cart and covered it with a large sack.

"Now it is my turn for a favour."

"Anything."

"I must visit the island. But my legs won't take me to your side of the walkway."

"Granny, I'll carry you there myself."

"That cart will do. Bring it tomorrow morning. Early…"

He was up before anyone else, sneaking to the shed to get the cart. The goat, tied up again in its stall, bleated at him but it still seemed a bit dazed. He hadn't counted on the cartwheels making so much noise on the cobbles and he couldn't see very well because he had no lantern. He had his story ready, though.

"Centurion's not happy with me. Says I have to go and clean the drains out down the road," he scowled.

Laughing, the guard opened a small door in the main gate. "Off you go then. Have fun."

Outside her house, he helped her onto the cart and covered her. Dragging it back over the bridge, he prayed to Mercury that no one was watching. He'd had enough of thinking up excuses. He hoped he wasn't jolting her too much. There wasn't much flesh on her to cushion the bumps. But, curled up under her long brown cloak, she made no complaint. When they reached the walkway, he helped her out onto the wet grass.

"Wait for me here," she said.

The voices were louder now.

"Vatta," they called, an insistent chorus that broke her concentration as she shuffled across. The river was lapping at the wooden piles supporting the walkway, sloshing up onto the walkway itself, making the logs slippery underfoot. Several times, she had to grab the swaying rope that stretched at hand height from the bank to the island. Pain shot up her legs and she stopped to steady herself with her stick. But she knew the Mothers would not let her fall.

At the shrine, it was clear to see why she had been summoned. The turbulent river had knocked over the small altar where the Mothers usually stood, had deposited weed, twigs and mud and carried away all the offerings.

"Let Vatta help you now as you have helped her in the past," she prayed.

From the small leather pouch slung over her shoulder, she took out a cloth, dipped it in a puddle and began to rub the faces of the three goddesses. She picked off the weed clinging to their hair, wiped mud off their clothes, smoothed grit from their feet. She righted the altar, brushed away twigs and soggy shreds of bark, then stood the Mothers in the centre.

Reaching back into the pouch, she took out a hairpin, the pretty one Dubnus had given her when their first child was born. So shiny, it was, with its smooth, round top. She placed it on the lap of the Mother holding a baby.

"Blessed Mothers. Watch over Brina when her time comes." She turned to go but then turned back. "And watch over that silly boy as well…"

What was she doing? Any moment, someone might see him on the riverbank. The guard thought he'd gone drain-cleaning. His bunkroom mates would be expecting him for training. And he still had to get her back to the settlement and himself over the bridge again without being spotted.

At last, there she was, wavering towards him. It wasn't just his haste to be away that made him stride over, pick her up in his arms and carry her to the bank. He settled her in the cart and wheeled her home at a run. As he lifted her out, she touched a hard-palmed hand to his face.

"Good boy. Don't worry. That goat won't give you any more trouble."

Mercury had helped him so far. He hoped the god would keep it up. He raced back over the bridge. The gate stood open now and he managed to get through by ducking in behind a wagon loaded with barrels and boxes. Back at the shed, he left the cart and patted the goat. Time to announce to everyone that Felix was well again.

He made it to the training yard just as the centurion was pairing the men off for sword practice.

"Just in time, lad. It was nearly drain-cleaning duties for you."

The others laughed and he grinned too before setting to work.

On his way back to the bunkroom at the end of the day, he called in at the smithy and bought one of the votive figures they made as a profitable sideline. A small lead goat. He planned to take it to the island and place it in Mercury's shrine as thanks. And tomorrow, he thought, he'd cross the river to visit the old woman and offer his help with repairing the walkway…

The Mothers were silent. Brina would deliver her child safely. And that silly boy was happy. Tes water seemed to have quietened too. The roaring had lessened and the flow of the river seemed calmer. She closed her eyes. She could rest now.

HIGHLY COMMENDED

ALICE AND GEORGE
YD JONES

The earth stirred. It didn't move, it didn't shake.

"There's something…" An indefinable essence moved within their being. There wasn't the slightest discernible noise, because sounds no longer meant anything in this world. The soil hadn't shifted for decades. Nought, nor no one disturbed their existence. Nothing changed.

"What lass, what'd you mean?"
 "I can feel something, there's something…"
 "Nay lass, there's nothing. There ain't been nothing this sixty, seventy years."
 "George, there's something!"
 "Rest, lass, you're being fanciful."
 "George, you're disturbing me. I can't rest when you're like this with me. It upsets me."

"Alice, lass, we've been together like this for longer than I would know. We don't utter nothing to each other no more, that's all gone for us now, lass, has been since… I don't remember when. I can't disturb you. How could I be disturbing you?"

"And yet, George love, you speak to me now."

A moment passed and George considered all that he knew.

"This is us now, Alice me love, we're here for all eternity, entwined, nought no more. My head next to yours, your arms within mine."

No words passed between them, no movement occurred, yet they knew each other's utterances.

"It's going, George, it's going. It's leaving me and I don't understand, but I don't think it should. I don't want it to."

"Let it go, Alice love, let it go. We don't need but you and me."

The essence of the 'something' faded away as Alice too drifted to that other place where she and George rested undisturbed, together, alone again.

•

Night came, and went. Days swirled past and the weather did its work. A little light rain, some broken clouds with sun struggling through now and again, until the grass started to grow with the vigour of spring. The tree above had dispensed with some of its more offensive little twigs, surplus to requirements, as new buds opened, thrusting with new growth. They collected in the shallow bowl below, which itself might have been unremarkable but for other debris blown and rolled into the earthy depression. Now there were bits of paper, faded strands of ribbon and the sun-scorched head of a plastic flower all now nestled safely, complicit with each other, sheltered from the elements.

A fragile kernel of recognition stirred Alice again.

"George," Alice tentatively mused, "George, it's happening again. I know it, I know this feeling. I know that I'm right."

George, always sensitive to his dear Yorkshire maid, slowly awoke to her bidding. Since Alice first roused him, George had become sentient. Just that, a fleeting consciousness he hadn't been subject to for decades. It came and went, and he was aware of Alice beside him then, their bones mingled, hers below his in the dark, dank earth some ten years until he'd joined her.

At the start he had been only too aware of her presence. Before it, he had longed for the time when he could be with his sweet Yorkshire lass, close enough to touch again, be in each other's embrace at last. When God above had decided, he had lain in his single bed in the small bedroom at the front of the old house. All his children had been, travelling from far and wide, and he understood, his time was soon. Of the thirteen children lovingly created, and the ten who'd survived, their firstborn William had travelled from Darlington prosperous and upstanding. He had stood at the foot of the bed, the late afternoon light through the tall High Street window, silhouetting him like an angel, radiating around the little room.

George's chest had constricted sharply as his eyes had become aware of the vision, and for a moment he'd sincerely wondered if this was his time to go. Then the bristles of William's fine moustaches came into focus and George was alerted to the reality, things were bad, still he lingered. They all came one by one, sometimes the girls together, watching over him, his angels to ease him to another world, not Gabriel and the heavenly hosts.

Some brought their children, if thought old enough, all weepy damp eyes and gangly. This saddened him the most, seeing the laughter and boldness drained from their gaunt war time faces. George was happy to be going, he'd missed Alice these ten years, the nearness, her warmth, and to be close to her in the blackness was his tired, aged ambition now.

When it finally happened, Rose had tended as usual. It was the night time and she'd placed the fresh gazunder in the usual place, put the water and the customary tot of whiskey within arms' length on the side table, the soda syphon next to the bed. Sitting on the edge of the bed that night, she was still visible despite the blackout. His gnarled fingers found hers with a gentle squeeze. She gave him some cheek the way she always did, her brazen impudence never far from the surface. There was a quiver in her voice this time, and it didn't seem to have the usual audacity, to send him to his sleep with a sense of affront and fight in his blood, to tick her off the next day. That girl! She had all her mother's spirit but not a drop of her sweetness or mothering, always a handful, but cheerfulness itself.

And then during that night, the silent stillness became thicker, breathing became sweeter, and fragrant within him. A drop of whiskey might shift this queer sense and he'd reached for the glass. Before his arm could be fully extended, he felt he was pushing through a thick warm wall. The stillness was absolute. He was in a cocoon, couldn't get out, not this time. For a moment he thought he sensed the murmuring of his mother's Cockney tongue, muttering gently, just out of hearing. A gentle coaxing reassurance. And then another tongue, sweetness itself. His eyes didn't see the shadows of the night anymore, they didn't see anything. He only felt the cloying honeyed sanctuary of warmth, the murmuring reassurance of his mother, the other voices growing stronger behind hers.

•

The clatter of the glass as it tumbled from the side table wasn't heard in the blackness, not found by Rose until the next morning when she checked on Dad. She hadn't noticed or missed it peeking in on the way to bed, distracted by the living in the blackout world, the visit of cousin Fred always an excitement.

But not to worry, George had been delivered into the

arms of Alice at last, the pain of his chest disseminated, the essence of his virility restored, and Alice's enfolding welcome there to greet him. He could not have described what had happened but he found himself swathed in love again, and had rested there these seventy five years, undisturbed in repose.

•

So now, to commune with Alice again after all this time? It triggered some perceptible effort he wasn't used to. But she was his Alice and he was her man, if she was inclined to be mindful of something, he'd comply with her fancies.

"Alice, lass, what is it, what's happening?"

"George, you know we was meant to be together, you and me, from the very start. From the moment we set eyes upon each other, the future was written. That day I saw you labouring near the Missus' house, I couldn't forget you. Your handsome face, no beard then, all lithe and stringy from the labour. I couldn't wait until the Missus would send me up the road on errands. I'd even hide things so I had to go out."

"I remember, the prettiest girl walking back and forth more times than I could count, until I got the chance to speak to you. I even hung around there that night so I could see you after you had finished work."

"I was lost in your blue eyes, George. Spellbound me they did, just like they do it on the variety stage." Alice giggled the sound of a hundred years past.

George was transported from the deep, cool earth where the bones of their once heaving chests intermingled now so you couldn't tell one from the other. Over the years George had slid and shifted as ice, snow and sodden earth had gently slipped him into Alice's embrace, his head resting next to hers, for all the world, kissing her gently on the cheek.

"Aye lass, I remember. That first time we got to be alone, when the Missus was away, and set the seal for the rest of our lives."

"The shame of it afterwards, but I wouldn't do anything differently. I couldn't."

"Nor I, my Yorkshire lass."

"You make me laugh, George, still calling me 'lass' after all this time, with your Cockney twang. Behaving for all the world like you think you're a Yorkshireman!"

"Where you are, I'll make my home, always have, always will." George's latterly softened London accent exaggerated to impress.

"You feel it too then? You feel the change?"

George conceded peacefully, he felt a change, something in the ether, if air they breathed at all.

How could it be? After those days of his passing when he realised Alice had been waiting, had welcomed him into the fissure of time and space she inhabited, both settled together intertwined for all time. How could it be they were communing now? Was it possible that there was movement in the atmosphere between them now? What had changed since he was placed below the cool wet earth, a barrier between them and that other place, where now they enjoyed freedom from pain, separation from the seasons of age, the stresses of life?

Something was altered, a change in the air. But what air can he speak of, air was no longer part of their world?

"I feel a change, a movement in our existence, George, that's all."

Nestled in each other, they remained in their joint being.

•

The stranger approached along the long central path, deeper into the oldest part, thoughts drifted through her mind. Memories of being sent from the school just over the old stone wall, by the teacher who'd instructed them to go make rubbings of old gravestones, only to be sent scarpering by the groundsman. They'd all secretly sniggered, when the dishy art teacher became aware of his error.

On another day they had congregated at the boys' end of the school yard, (it was so unfair they needed the largest part to play football). The girls, told to gather by the old wall for the netball team photograph, and at a loose end for a while had all hung over the old wall. This was the first time they had the chance to observe the mysteries of the old cemetery. Unattended, they strained their eyes at the beautiful, mournful statues and headstones. So many children.

"Look at that one, she was only seven years old."

"Have you seen that angel, a baby one year old, and a brother only three months?"

As the stranger arrived half way in, looking again to that corner, vexation rumbled deep in her stomach again. Not only the school gone, but the groundsmen and all the headstones and angels that told of saddened parents' forlorn grief. How could they do that, how could they just eliminate and strike from the ground the memory of those children, replaced with a glib sign, 'Place of rest of numerous un-named children'? They weren't un-named and never were. She remembered, her friends remembered, outraged, their remembrance scraped from the earth. Probably easier for the council grass cutter to turn round.

Continuing along the central pathway, so many of the stately, carefully chosen tomb stones removed, it scarcely retained its original sombre completeness of earlier days. Towards the end at the ground level tap, she turned right along the grassy now unpaved path. Always careful to remain on the pathway, never disrespected the resting inhabitants. Another cut, silently sniping, why bother to repair the old pavings, just remove and sling in a skip. Grass will do for these inhabitants.

At the hollow under the big tree, she stopped and placed the implements around her feet.

"George, George, it's there again, that stirring in my stomach again."

"Alice love, you're speaking of things we know nothing of no more. What stomach, lass, what do you mean?" George's pained concern was clear. He had accommodated Alice's notions, had even wondered if he comprehended her utterings, but where was she going with this, he worried for her.

But then, he wondered… he was concerned for her reasoning, how could that even be possible? He was communicating with her, he was challenging her rationality. It passed as he fell into empty contemplation, the moment expanding into a different consciousness of perception. A stretching of being, of awareness, an emerging of presence.

"George, my love, do you feel it now?" Alice knew her winsome words could reach him this time. He wasn't just placating his beloved any more, she felt his awareness, could feel what he too sensed. When he spoke again he would know himself.

•

Above their caressing hearts, the woman knelt to the ground, the warmth of her body permeated the coolness of the surface grass. As her knee touched the ground, a wisp of something curled from the thinly clothed flesh and pervaded the upper level of earth. An unhurried wave of being started to ease through the wormholes and crevices of undisturbed earth, descending, branching and reaching to the edges of their existence. Her other knee dropped and shifted a handful of loose earth as a second tendril pressed through the surface mud and pushed on down, splitting and spreading, the weight from seventy five years of dense peaceful earth no resistance.

A gloved hand reached down into the detritus and scooped up waste paper and twigs. Again and again the fingers worked, raking from further and further apart to gather in the centre and scoop the debris from eons of neglect, warm coils of being continuing to delve ever downward.

The hollow began to resemble the surrounding cleanly clipped grass of the cemetery, nearly all the rubbish carefully placed in a plastic bag until eventually only small pieces of dead leaves and twiglets remained. Throwing off her leather gloves to the side, the woman carefully picked through the grass to clean the area thoroughly. In an unaccountable, sudden abandoned gesture, she leaned forward, spreading her two bare hands upon the cleansed grass, feeling the cool earth beneath her.

Oblivious to the gathering energy, plunging deeper and warmer beneath her, the woman carefully created a small flower bed to the head of the grave. Beneath her, the gentle familial bonds of the woman unconsciously caressed those below. Alice and George's dry old bones recognised the cherished emotions of their visitor, both giving themselves up to this new actuality, tenderly combining, embracing, reaching towards the woman, at one, together.

•

Many years had passed since. The woman continued to visit regularly, and as she moved around the cemetery, curiously arriving at an ever increasing family circle, Alice and George joining her arm in arm, directing her in the sunshine. Here Samuel, nineteen years, only son, lost in an RAF landing accident on British soil only months before the end of the war. There Alice and George's youngest grandson Arthur and his young wife Mae, childless, content to remain undisturbed together alone, such was their love.

For the woman as she meandered the pathways, she had the mystifying notion of an accompanying warmth promenading in tandem with her, just out of touch. Not Samuel or Arthur, there were no longer any connection for them, parents gone, no others to follow, all peaceful in their place of rest. The ethereal, tender loving eyes of Alice and George glanced towards Rose's grand-daughter. For all her heedless lifestyle, she had done them proud.

•

Sometimes, Alice and George would take a stroll along the old pathways of their youth in the adjoining park, alone. They could see the flowerbeds of their heyday, full to the borders with overflowing exquisite flowers of their memories, sunshine on their backs, sunbeams bouncing off the vivid colours. Shadowy strangers walked with dogs through the flowerbeds oblivious to their beauty, children chasing balls. As Alice placed her arm in the crook of his, he placed his hand upon hers, content with their lot, in the warm sunshine, eternally happy.

HIGHLY COMMENDED

CROSSING THE TEES
CHITRA KUMARI

"Nani, time to go for a walk." Alisha was at the door.

"I am ready, let me take my raincoat," Sheela replied.

"The weather is not bad, Nani, come on, we are getting late." She was getting impatient.

Sheela loved her walk with her granddaughter; she used to cherish every second of her company. Alisha was a bright girl in her teens, young, energetic and full of life. She had taken the responsibility to take her out for a walk every evening since Sheela had moved to Barnard Castle. Both loved walking along the River Tees.

"You are walking very slow today. What's the matter, Nani?" Alisha stopped and looked at her face. Her grandma did not look very happy today, there was something strange, making her face appear gloomy, something she was trying to hide.

"It's my arthritis, my joints are getting stiff. But you

don't worry. As I take more steps, it would start easing. It's strange, isn't it?" she continued. "I become stiff when I sit too long but what to do, can't walk all the time I am stiffening up!" She tried to smile but it was a strange smile mixed with sadness.

"Why not? You can go for a walk in the morning, again after lunch. These would keep you fit!" She had always encouraged her to go out alone and spend time outdoor rather than sitting all alone inside the house. "You would make friends as well if you try."

"I feel awkward walking alone in my Indian clothes."

"Silly you, no one bothers what you are wearing. But you can wear trousers, I think you would need it in the winter, it would feel very cold otherwise. I know you cannot bear cold."

"Wouldn't I look fat with my big bum in the trousers? But I would try."

Alisha smiled. "Please do try, Nani." She held her Nani's hand to comfort her and both continued their walk. The sun disappeared under the cloud, the sky turned grey, cool wind started blowing. The weather had changed.

The sound of the flowing water in the River Tees was taking them to a tranquil depth of thinking. Both were quiet, lost in their own world. Alisha was thinking of her school, still holding her Nani's hand.

"The sound of flowing water in your River Tees reminds me of our River Ganga. I grew up on the bank of River Ganga."

Alisha did not like 'your' river and 'our' river. How can

she feel like this? Rivers are nature's gift, they belong to everyone. But she did not argue with her Nani, she let her speak, keeping her view to herself.

"Our River Ganga is very big. In monsoon it swells up as if going to submerge the earth. You know my mother always told us to worship the river, Ma Ganga as told. We never prayed but she did every day. She used to light the candle, offered flowers and prayed on the bank of river for our safety and wellbeing."

"That's funny, a river cannot be Almighty God, and how would a river protect you? These are all superstitions."

"I knew you would say so but my mother always said Ganga is our mother, mother of all those living on her bank, her holy water is our strength, her land is our wealth. We should thank her and take her blessings by offering our prayers. If she got angry, she would submerge our village and would take us under her deep water."

"Nani, do you really believe all this? You were a science student." Alisha looked straight into her eyes waiting for her reply. Her Nani appeared to be lost in a different world. She was nowhere near her. She appeared to have gone too far, possibly on the bank of the River Ganga. She was not now on the River Tees. Her look frightened Alisha, and she shook her shoulders. "Nani, where are you lost?"

"How can I dare to not to believe all this?" Her voice was weak. She was trembling. "My brother drowned the day my mother did not worship Ma Ganga. She had forgotten to go to the bank to offer her prayer." Tears were rolling down her face, she could not hold herself, she broke down.

Alisha was stunned. She had never seen her grandma like that. She wanted to change the topic. "Shall we cross the bridge today? Are your legs okay?"

Sheela nodded. She was quiet now, her face under the shadow of the grief and old memories.

Alisha wanted to ask about her brother but she didn't. It was not the right time.

As they crossed the River Tees, she noticed her grandma stop in the middle of the bridge, look down for a moment, then bring out a red rose from her purse and a coin, that she dropped in the river, whispering something with her folded hand.

She was praying. "Om Shanti, Om Shanti."(*Almighty God I pray for peace*).

They stood there for a few minutes and finally Sheela broke her silence. "Seventy years ago, on this date, my brother drowned in the River Ganga. He was a good swimmer but the river took him. My mother died a week later with the guilt that she lost her son because she forgot to worship Ma Ganga."

Alisha hugged her grandma. Both were in tears, their tears were dropping in the River Tees. The sun suddenly reappeared from the midst of the clouds, spreading warmth and light. On the other side of the bridge, the silvery trunks of birch trees were reflecting the sun to make patterns on the grass below.

SHORTLISTED STORIES

A BRIDGE BETWEEN STRANGERS
MICHAEL ATKINSON

The diesel engine with the short carriages in tow rolled to a slow stop at the Teesside platform. A pre-recorded voice spoke gently through the grey speaker that was mounted above the cabin doorway; it announced the arrival at Thornaby station. A diverse mix of daylight commuters vacated their seats, full of politeness as they squeezed past the standing passengers. The gentleman in the navy blue uniform stood guard on the concrete slabs, kindly prompting people to mind the gap as they off loaded in an orderly fashion. Health and safety was his primary concern as the working rush was about to begin. His metallic whistle hung proudly from a white neck loop; it was clear he was eager to blast it as the last body hopped off.

The electronic clock with its large red digits overhung the terminal gateway. It somehow had influence and control over the smartly dressed characters that Joe shared his journey with. He would often see them gripping their briefcase handles like a relay baton as if the country depended on them claiming a gold medal. Although, it would only ever be themselves taking part in the morning race, briskly running towards the exit as their polished brogue shoes slapped against the station's tiled floor. Their real competition of course, was sales statistics, slogging away all day, meeting targets, making money for the people above.

Those who wore rucksacks and loose clothing appeared to be immune to the ascending numbers. They were the people that took a more casual approach to their leave, some stopped for a morning shot of coffee, others wandered across to the paper merchants to buy the freshly printed news, and the last remaining few often stood, littering the area as they twiddled their thumbs against the screens of mobiles phones. Joe was one of those coffee drinkers. He would buy his small luxury every morning, for the same amount, at the same time and from the same stand.

After parting with gold and silver change, he took hold of his cardboard cup, ascended up a level and made his way onto the main street.

The Monday morning weather was in a considerably good mood. Any blues for an early start to the working week stood no chance as Joe hovered at the junction, waiting to cross as the rising sun beat down upon his face. He adjusted his black framed glasses, scratched his dark trimmed beard and took a sip from the morning potion. Cars pulled up to the painted white line as the lights changed to a fiery red; it portrayed the burning attitude of workers trapped in the work to live cycle, allowing Joe to safely cross to the other side.

Taking in the awakening scenery, he observed a row of fishermen that sat proudly on little, blue folding stools by the riverbank. Their rods were held firmly, ready to jump into action at the sight of a disappearing bobbing orange tip. Ready to throw their hand around the ball bearings like a gatling gun. Furiously winding until the watery prize was revealed.

Heading towards the footbridge, Joe adjusted the beige satchel across his left shoulder, glancing at his watch in doing so. Plenty of time, he thought to himself.

Starting at nine was a doddle. Working backstage at the local theatre was a relaxed job on most occasions. It was only on select evenings when he really had to work for his money, organising backdrops, props and taking charge of theatre maintenance. He had acquired plenty of experience over the years whilst he had been working there. He saw it as his. Things ran smoothly when he was on duty.

Making his way to the suspended bridge, Joe took another sip of the hot drink and marched up the steps ready to cross the River Tees. The Millennium Bridge was a beautiful piece of engineering, a real treat to walk across and admire the stretched views up and down the river. The hanging walkway softly bounced in line with the tempo of the walking beat. It was a joint effort of around twelve composers crossing the waterway to conduct the swaying rhythm.

Joe's eyes widened and his lips pursed together.

It was at the other end of the bridge that Joe could see the blonde woman wearing the green coat coming his way. He pressed his mouth against the thin plastic lid and slowly tilted the cup. Taking a drink, he started to go through all the possibilities of his upcoming actions.

Joe knew himself that he was not a confident man. After being bullied through his school and college years, he often avoided social interaction with strangers, especially women.

Yet, since having the chance of sitting in on one of the motivational talks about confidence a few weeks ago, at the age of twenty nine he decided that it was time to put his past behind him and take charge of his life. He wanted to make the most of every situation presented before him, start to say yes instead of coming up with excuses and reasons not to attend uncomfortable gatherings.

His hands became slightly damp as he drew closer with each step. She was unaware, but he had seen her every weekday for the last nine weeks. He always cautiously peeked out the side of his lenses as they passed in opposite directions. Joe secretly admired her golden mane that matched her fair skin in the few seconds of close proximity. She always wore the same green coat, small black ankle boots with the little gold buckles and always had her eyes buried into a thin book. Roughly judging her around the same age, it was Joe's moment of perfection he looked forward to each morning.

This is it, Joe told himself.

With his free hand twisting and fiddling with the corded satchel strap strewn across his torso, he took a final sip of courage ready to speak in the world of the unknown. Adrenaline started to release through his body as he felt both arms become heavy. Locking his eyes onto the beautiful target, his chest filled with air as they reached the centre of the bridge.

"Morning," Joe cheerfully exclaimed, keeping his warm personality on show as he approached.

Captured by the words in her book, the woman did not acknowledge him. The green coated hornet continued on her flight path across the river, completely oblivious to his efforts.

Joe's valiant attempt came crashing down on top of him, crushing his dream for an easy introduction, obliterating his confidence, extinguishing his hope of striking up a conversation. Staring at his onward pacing feet, he tried to process what just happened. Rejection, exclusion and dismissal. How could simple ignorance cause this cyclone of emotions. His hidden thoughts cast a darkened cloud as he stepped down from the river crossing.

Walking through the theatre doors, Joe clenched his fist, crumpling and destroying the stiff cardboard cup, ploughing it into the recycling bin. He signed into his work station and advanced to check his daily duties. A vicious scowl appeared upon his face. It was a list of props that needed moving from stage to warehouse storage. It was just the mundane task he required to bring him back down to where he thought he belonged. His miserable portrait was a result from the internal storm of boiling anger.

As the hours ticked by, he kept to himself for the remainder of his shift. He even found a secluded spot amongst the decommissioned stage lighting to eat his late lunch. His mind still adjusting from the public outcasting. He slouched and queried over what to do next, but of course, no inspiration came his way. He put himself back into work mode and finished filing and storing boxes.

The time was once again at five. He clocked himself out and exited the building. He dreaded every step he took. Having to face and cross the bridge of humiliation ladened him with an uncomfortable feeling he learnt from the morning. Busier this time, he joined a larger crowd and stepped up for his return crossing. Mingling at the back of workers, he looked onwards over shoulders.

There she was again, the green hornet coming back for a second sting. Joe walked closer to the back of the group, stooping his shoulders, lowering his neck, hiding his face for protection. His hidden safety net however, quickly disappeared. The group of happy workers veered left down a footpath towards a small pub that was opening its doors, ready to intake the sobers and roll them out as drunks. Joe was left fully exposed. He looked around for an escape route but had no choice but to cross the river.

A quickened heart rate slowed his feet. The coated woman kept her sturdy pace, eating up the distance between them. Joe couldn't believe he had to pass her again. Their collision course was inevitable.

With no pre-empting of consequences, he delved into a hidden pocket of courage and tried one last time to strike a conversation with the stranger.

Closer this time, he gave a small, timid wave. "Hello," he said in a nervous tone.

The woman's eyes averted from the printed text. She looked up with slight confusion as she kept walking. She gave Joe a brief look and analysed the expression he wore. No response again, that was it for him, confirmation of his failure. His sight fixed to the ground in front of him and he focused on one thing, getting home and shutting out the world.

Her book snapped shut, words crashed together, the pages slapped against each other, trapping a dusky pink marker inside that poked out from several chapters in. Sliding it into her handbag, she turned and walked energetically in Joe's direction to catch him up.

The dull tone of his footsteps continued as he neared the end of the bridge. Grabbing the handrail, he felt a gentle tapping on his shoulder. Natural instinct made his head turn to the unfamiliar but pleasant sensation.

He looked on in confusion.

The woman he had been admiring for so long was standing before him, graciously waving her hands in a rhythmical sequence. Joe did not know what to do in response to her actions, although no words came from her mouth, her hands told it all. It was clear why the morning efforts went unnoticed. The cold woman he thought she once was, now appeared in a warming light. Pointing to her ear, he understood the word she mouthed.

"Oh, sorry, I didn't know," Joe explained as the realisation for his lack of knowledge into the deaf world was non-existent.

The woman smiled back, trying to put his panicked state at ease. She reached into her handbag and pulled out a small pad of post-it notes accompanied by a ball point pen. Almost as if she had done this before, she jotted something onto the small square and tore it off. Handing over the brightly coloured paper tile, Joe examined her handwriting and gave a gentle smile back.

"Kate," he announced.

She nodded her head and proceeded to write another message for him to read. Joe's anxiety was a mix of nerves and excitement, a cocktail of shaken adrenaline, something that he had never really felt before. He waited, holding onto the handrail of the bridge, eager to read the next installment. Kate presented another pink square for him to read. Taking it between his thumb and index finger, he examined the text.

"I am deaf, sorry I did not hear you!"

In the moments that Joe was reading her note, he was frantically trying to find a process for the next possible set of actions. Stalling a little, taking a little longer to observe her writing, he drew a blank. He managed to strike up the conversation that he had hoped for, but had no way of keeping its fluency.

Stumbling for his words, he did the only thing that came to his mind, speak his name. "My name is Joe."

A puzzled look emerged with Kate as she shook her head from side to side, locks of golden hair washed over her shoulders back and forth. She handed him her black pen and a clean square. Joe knew instantly that he would have to communicate his message through scribbled font. Using his hand as a makeshift easel, he finished off his name and tried his best to draw an artistic smiley face.

His contemporary and spontaneous piece of artwork produced a wide grin across Kate's face as she read his message. Neatly folding his post-it and placing it in her book, she checked her watch and scrawled another message to hand to him.

"Have to catch bus! See you tomorrow!"

Sticking his thumb up, he nodded and smiled, agreeing to the next brief encounter before his Tuesday stint of work started. Kate, of course conjured something a lot more fluent, somewhat majestic and certainly more tasteful than a single thumb. Her hands flowed with vibrancy, it was mesmerising to watch, even though Joe did not understand one bit of what he saw.

Parting with shy waves, they once again set foot in opposite directions. His mind was supercharged. As he bound himself for the station, he could feel the valves release what seemed like nitrous oxide gushing through his system. This was surely a good feeling, Joe tried to convince himself. Trying to mentally plot the sensation of fainting and delirium on a imaginary venn diagram, he placed himself exactly in the overlapping intersection. The smell of the familiar diesel fumes and electric current brought Joe's mind back into the authentic world.

The metal doors slid open and out came the same proud owner of that shiny whistle. The pre-recorded message informed the passengers of their outbound journey. Joe was oblivious to the noise, he even looked around wondering where his return coffee had been placed. Unnaturally, he had completely missed the fresh vendor and boarded without completing his homeward tradition. This would have certainly caused some form of misery as he endured glum and tired faces sat in the opposite seats, however on this occasion, as he sat re-reading the pink squares over and over again, his temperament was calm and somewhat peaceful.

As the carriage wheels tore along the track, he dislodged his smart phone from the shallow pocket on his jeans. Locating the search engine, his fingers proceeded to tap the glass in an organised pattern, letters turning to words, words turning to phrases. He clicked the blue search button and scrolled through a variety of results. Finding what looked like suitable reading material, he double tapped with the tip of his finger and started to study the phone screen in more detail.

I can do this, he thought to himself again. Starting with A, his hands matched the demonstrators on the screen. Okay, easy enough, he reflected internally. B, a different handshape, a little more complex than the first one he tried. C, he was starting to get the hang it. Determined to learn at least the alphabet in sign language before his next meeting, he persevered, all the way through his return trip and even whilst walking to his front door. By nightfall, Joe had the twenty five letters mastered. Able to spell names with his fingers and even spell out words, he was slightly confident that he could slowly spell out short phrases in the air that would hopefully make sense to Kate. Just in case he failed miserably, he decided to pack a sketchpad and blue pen into his work bag as a back up. At almost midnight, Joe was unaware of the time, wrapped up in a new excitement, he had to cool the turbos and switch off. Try and rest for the early morning start.

It was a restless night, presumably due to the nerves of unknowing, but the alarm clock had no sympathy. Six am came around and the electronic orchestra played out loudly. Silenced and reset, his morning routine had begun. Clothes ironed, lunch packed and station targeted. The mundane cycle of the morning commute was always the same. The recorded voice, the shiny whistle, the relay race and the aroma of coffee. Today was different, Joe had something other than a single purpose of working, it was the day he broke through the barrier he faced yesterday.

The morning fishermen, still sat in the same pitch, often made Joe wonder if they actually went home or camped out to secure the prime feeding spot.

Stepping up a further time, crossing to the centre of the Tees, he eagerly waited, tapping his fingers against the metal rail as he looked down over the river. Checking his watch, she was right on cue. Coming his way, this time the slim book already tucked away in the sandy coloured bag hanging across her body. Kate gave a gentle wave and Joe mirrored one back. Raising his hands as she came and stood close, he produced the finger pattern he had been working on last night. J-O-E. His efforts seemed to have impressed her, more so than the attempt at the smiley artwork previously. Slight wrinkles appeared under her eyes as she smiled widely. Kate rummaged into her bag and pulled out the pink post-its. Wondering what she could be writing, he waited and pondered what his next set of finger sequences could spell.

Kate insisted as she handed him the coloured square to read.

"Coffee? Tonight 5:30? Bar Ceno?"

Looking at the coffee cup she had drawn on the bottom, he could tell her artistic skills towered his. Putting competition aside, he gave a friendly smile and raised his fingers once more. Sequencing them, Kate understood the word he spelt, Y-E-S.

LA QUESTION FRANCAISE
JULIE BAGGOTT

I haven't given an immediate answer therefore Sylvie Dupont puts the question another way. She looks to be in her early forties, blonde highlighted hair brushing the shoulders of her expensive pin-striped blue trouser suit. It brings out the colour of her piercing blue eyes which are clear and encouraging. I don't feel wrong footed but consider how to articulate the answer professionally and succinctly.

I worked over Christmas. Nobody wants to work then so it's difficult running a hotel and trying to be as fair as possible to staff, whilst keeping up an excellent standard of service and I prided myself on excellence. I stand about five foot three but I was used to projecting a much larger presence. I kept my long chestnut hair pulled back in a severe bun and my green eyes flashed with alertness, never missing a trick. I always wore a black trouser suit. I had been hotel manager for the Marriott hotel in Canary Wharf for five years and I had worked hard. I hadn't been home during this time. I rang my mother once a week on a Sunday afternoon. She understood that my hours weren't very flexible but always stressed she would "welcome a visit". I was her only child and since my father had been killed in a car crash seven years previously, she had had to manage alone. She was a strong woman, physically and mentally and I had never had any worries about her until I received a phone call from a Macmillan nurse on the second of January.

"Sophie, I'm afraid your mother is in the last stages of lung cancer. I think it's advisable you come home."

"How long do you think she has?"

"The doctor is reckoning on about two weeks."

I was shocked. Mum had given me no indication that she was suffering. I had tried to encourage her to give up smoking when I gave up ten years previously but she had claimed it was "one of her pleasures in life". Of course I had to return home and spend her last hours with her. I organised a rota with my assistant manager and heads of departments and left London the following morning to arrive in Stockton on Tees by midday.

As I let myself in to 17 Grange Road, the home where I had been brought up, I could sense a feeling of fragility as if the molecules of air were being sucked in and out of death's rattling throat. I chastised myself severely for my five year absence – my negligence. I could hear someone speaking softly from a bedroom upstairs and the creak of floorboards as she walked around the bed. I left my luggage in the hall and climbed the stairs with trepidation.

My mother's eyes were closed when I entered the room but she opened them as I introduced myself to Angela, the nurse who was sitting in an easy chair to the right of the bed. Angela was about thirty six and rotund. Her short, brown hair curled up at the ends. Her deep brown eyes mirrored empathy. My mother smiled weakly, whispered my name, then her eyelids fluttered shut again and she slept. Her usually bright and sparkling green eyes were covered and her white permed hair flattened against the pillow. She was dressed in a clean full length flowery nightdress. Angela accompanied me downstairs to the kitchen where she made us a cup of tea.

"She wants to die in her own home, Sophie. That is her wish."

"But what can we do?" I asked trembling.

"Just make her as comfortable as possible during her last days. She'll be grateful you're here."

"But I didn't know."

"It was only discovered in its very late stages. She knew how busy you were and didn't want to be a burden."

"But she's my mum."

I wondered how selfish I had been or blinkered. When my dad died, I had thrown myself into work. I'd had a coil of negativity spiralling upwards inside me that had threatened to choke my thinking and suffocate my mind. Hours and days of darkness had been kept at bay by overseeing functions and arguing with the head housekeeper over laundry bills when I was an assistant hotel manager. I'd engaged my energy in working my way up to being the General Manager. This had consumed me. When I called my mother she seemed to be coping. She spent time with friends and involved herself with the local Women's Institute. She wasn't dwelling on her sorrow. Would the darkness threaten me now? I was to be left alone. No family and no one in London to call a friend. I had been so eager to climb the ladder I had spent no time forming personal relationships, only colleagues.

I kept a vigil at my mother's bedside, reading to her from women's magazines and administering water when she indicated throatily that she was thirsty. I slept in the easy chair next to her bed. Angela kept us company. It was a miserable few weeks but I wouldn't have wanted to be anywhere else. I reproached myself continually for my long absence. I had been so caught up in work. I'd never even contemplated anything could happen to mum. She was only sixty two. It seemed inconceivable.

I awoke with a jolt in the last week of January. It was a Friday, I think. I could hear Angela in the kitchen. Looking at mum, I knew she had gone. Her chest was still and she felt cold as I kissed her cheek.

"Goodbye, mum," I said, the emotion catching at my throat then I called Angela from the top of the stairs.

The organisation of the funeral kept me busy for a week. We had no family. Mum and dad had been only children and I had no brothers or sisters. Friends attended and members of mum's WI. I was also abundantly grateful to her WI for putting on the spread at her wake and for getting permission for me to use their meeting room at the community hall for the event.

The funeral went well. As I drew up to my childhood home in a taxi, exhaustion and sorrow hit me. I let myself in and went straight to my mother's bedroom, empty and spiritless. I curled up on the bed and sobbed. My wretched tears continued until after midnight when I fell into a fitful sleep, dreaming of my mother as I had seen her five years ago, beautiful and wondrous. In my imagination she shone as if belonging to an angelic realm. I kept reaching out trying to take her hand but she danced, shimmering, leading me through an enchanted woodland.

I woke at six in the morning, cold, on top of the duvet and went downstairs to make a cup of tea, missing Angela. The big question was what to do with myself. I felt aimless and discouraged. I didn't have the fire in me to return to London and I knew I had already overspent the compassionate leave I had been allowed. How long would it take me to get a job in Stockton – something to take my mind off this?

I decided it wouldn't take very long to get a temping position by signing up to a few agencies in the area. Work would be almost immediate. I went to a couple of agencies and did the tests. Work arose two weeks later. There was a job going at Cubic that was administrative and would suit my needs. It involved data entry which was monotonous and mindless but it kept me occupied.

A routine developed which carried my bruised soul.

I walked from home to work and back again. I walked into the centre of town, followed steps down to the river when I would walk at the riverside, then up a flight of steps that led to a bridge that crossed the Tees over to the Cubic building on the opposite bank. As I walked to work, I walked with the flow of the wide river. As I walked home from work, I walked against the flow of the river. Sometimes as I was crossing the Tees, I would stop on the bridge and look down, feeling the steady, unceasing flow of the mighty body of water. My journey came to symbolise the spirit of the North East. This surging river with its stoic flow embodied the people of this area, a life force running through them, a never ending joie de vivre despite hardships and ill fortune, an optimism that belied the difficult times they had experienced and continued to do so. By the river, over the river, I felt grounded in an identity that suffused through me. It was part of me, always had been and always would be wherever I lived, with whomever I mixed. I had strength and vitality to carry on. My mum had lived with the spirit of the North and I could see her rising out of the water, leading me forwards, in my dreams. She had never given in. The water was life-giving, nourishing, clear. I felt a sense of belonging that had evaded me before now. Home was home. I had connected with something tangible, although the water would pour through my fingers. I still had a way to go.

On an evening when the sky was ready to unleash

droplets the size of penny pieces, I bumped into Mrs Thompson. I had been best friends with her daughter at school. I hadn't stayed in touch with Rachel just like I hadn't with anyone, being so fixated with work. Mrs Thomson hadn't known my mum had died and offered her sympathy. Rachel had gone to university she told me and landed herself a job in Cannes as an Events Organiser. She was always very busy her mum informed me. I told Mrs Thomson I was just getting back on my feet. Just as torrents began to fall, she handed me a card.

"Here, Sophie, this has Rachel's email address on it. I'm sure she'd love to hear from you."

Sixteen years had passed since school but I must admit, I was curious and we had been very close. I made sure the card was protected from the weather by inserting it into a pocket in my purse. Mrs Thomson gave me a hug and we parted, each of us smiling in the face of the downpour.

Spring was beginning to coyly reveal itself; the temperature was milder and buds were appearing on the stark skeletal trees. I still hadn't emailed Rachel. I wasn't sure what to say nor how she'd react. I had taken a morning off work to see the dentist for a six monthly check up. Waiting to be seen, I picked up a copy of The Lady magazine. I flicked through the articles, skimmed through the positions vacant for au pairs, then my eyes were drawn to a half page advertisement for managers for a holiday complex in the South of France. The complex comprised of camping sites and hotels in Frejus. I felt a stirring of interest. When I left the dentists, I asked the receptionist if I could take the magazine with me. I offered to pay but she said there was no problem, I could have it.

As my excitement grew, so did my doubts. Why would I want to go to France? What would I find there that I couldn't find here? Friends perhaps, a whole new culture, a sunnier climate. Now that I had found my spiritual bearings in Stockton, I felt I could go anywhere and make a home. I was settled in me. If I needed to come back to Stockton, I always could. I had the strength absorbed from my surroundings to carry me and the attitude of the region to keep me going. I decided I would apply for the job.

The interviews are taking place in Manchester and I have been called to interview. There are three of us, two men and myself. They entered the small function room of the Mancunian Mal Maison hotel before me. Their interviews lasted about forty minutes each. I go in about 11.30am.

I am surprised there is only one lady in the room. She introduces herself as CEO of the company who just happened to be in Manchester and has therefore agreed to carry out the interviews. Normally she wouldn't do this but she is interested in the new recruits. Her name is Sylvie Dupont. She looks me over. I am wearing a light grey skirt suit and have left my hair loose to cascade down my back. I wear just enough make up and a subtle perfume. She stands up and shakes my hand firmly over the desk that separates us.

"I'm very pleased to meet you Sophie and wow! Your CV is amazing," she says.

I look at my hands modestly, then back at her, meeting her eyes as she goes through my CV.

"What's the impetus for moving to France, Sophie?" she asks.

That's the question.

"I'm ready for a change and I feel the opportunity will offer many new challenges." I have answered professionally but then I decide to add something that is more from a humane angle.

"I like the idea of working with a team of other managers, forming relationships, and I have a good friend who lives in Cannes."

"How helpful," she answers. She continues, "Well Sophie, I was absolutely knocked out by your CV so meeting you was just a formality. I'd decided I would offer you one of the positions if I liked the look of you and I do like the look of you. I have no reservations in offering you the job. Think it over and get back to me by the end of the week."

I email Rachel that evening. I write about what I have been doing since school and inform her of the new job opportunity. She emails back the same night that I absolutely "must" take the job. She says France is "heavenly" and it would be great to be so close to each other. I needn't have worried about her reaction. I hope we just fall in and carry on where we left off.

I put the house on the market and leave the business of

selling it to the estate agents. I hand in my notice at Cubic. I am packed and ready to go. The taxi is picking me up at 11am. I was up at 7am and take one last walk to the river. A steady and unceasing flow lifts me just to watch it. This is the compass of my heartland. This is where I have been bred and born but I am starting a new adventure. The river flows through me, fulfills and renews me, draws me homewards, casts me onwards.

THE PAGE WITH NOTHING ON IT
SUE BAXTER

The light fluctuated between browns, greens as it stretched its body fluidly, flicking through the water using tailfin and flipper to glide into patches, which every now and then were streaked with silver and gold lights

A boy sat by a wall staring at an empty sheet of paper in the book he was holding. The wheeled go-cart he had built himself was beside him.

Another boy nearby picked up small stones, placed them in a sling and whirled them around his head. One flew out of the sling and bounced off the wall, hitting the other boy on the head.

Disturbed from the reverie (on nothing that he had before him) he looked up angrily at the other boy who then ran off.

The injured boy jumped in his cart and pursued him downhill. When he turned abruptly, the cart was unable to accommodate the sudden change and continued on... and on... Unable to stop he was thrown over the edge, tumbling onto the riverbank, where he lay stunned.

Sinuously sliding through the currents of water, evading fronds of leathery weed in feathered sea strands, it propelled itself effortlessly into undulating gold reflections where silver fish darted enticingly. Tiring of this, it heaved itself onto the muddy bank and lay there.

Many hours may have passed, when the boy noticed a large immobile rock that was close to him. This rock became not so immobile. In fact its tailfins began to extend and seem like legs. Eventually a rotund figure wearing a dark brown suit and top hat made its way towards him.

The boy watched as the large dark brown eyes encased in horn-rimmed glasses regarded him.

The man noticed the wreckage of wood and wheels that surrounded the figure lying on the bank. He also noticed a page of paper ripped from a book.

"What's written on that?" he said, to which the boy replied, "Nothing."

The man picked the paper up and proceeded to read from it. Meanwhile the air seemed to ripple like water, although to the boy the surroundings seemed more and more like a library. The stranger read from the paper.

"Yet with the enhancement of sight, enabled by glass curved into a lens, that which had seemed only blackness revealed a prick of light which became known as Uranus. Whereupon this prick of light known as Uranus itself revealed, by consulting the description of an ellipse that it was not in its prescribed orbit. In one place it appeared to be ahead, in another behind, in its anticipated path. Although no other body could be seen, its presence had been felt – in time this other body became known as Neptune…"

"So you're interested in astronomy?" said the stranger to the boy in the library who appeared to be becoming less and less distinct. His outline appeared to be wobbling like jelly. "There's a book on astronomy on that shelf up there."

He pulled a library ladder over and climbed up to reach it.

The boy watched as the man climbed up the rusty ladder that led onto the quay, from which he ambled down a lamplit street. Before he had left the riverbank he had seen the boy turn into a shoal of fish and swim downstream.

MAKING WAVES
S.A BOON

I slid my tan brogue forward just close enough to feel the euphoria mix with fear, the quick shifting waters below asking the question, is today the day? My reverie was soon shattered by a message reaching my phone. It was Martha: *"Need help with the assignment, can you meet me by the fire?"* My gut said no, tell the bitch to do it herself, but that's not me as far as anyone's concerned. As far as they know, I'm polite and well meaning if not a little uptight. Standing there at the water's edge with the cold wind whipping my face, I agreed to meet Martha. I guess today wasn't the day after all.

I was now in the Thomas Sheraton for the second time this week warming my hands by the fire, my life now held together by tenuous threads I didn't care to fathom. Martha's face was lit up as she outlined the plot to her latest short film, her voice filled with childish naivety: "…and it ends with them finding each other in the crowd and 'she' proposes."

My eyes rolled like two eight balls.

"Jesus, Martha, why is it always so neatly tied up? That's not life, that's not the way. It should end with her lost in the crowd, realising he just wanted to fuck her!" Worrying I'd revealed too much of myself, I stopped short to look back at Martha.

With her eyes holding two fat droplets, she sobbed. "It's crap, isn't it? I can tell you don't like a bit of it."

Though I was nothing but honest with her clichéd plot lines and hammy characters, I decided it appropriate to comfort her. In the last few years I felt all of my lectures and criticisms landed on dull ears; I wasted precious time on inane women who wanted nothing more than to be reality stars and talking air-heads. Not since Sally has there been anyone who truly grasped my ideas, but now wasn't the time to catch that train.

I placed my hand on Martha's knee and handed her a napkin.

"I'll help you think of a more dramatic ending, don't worry. At least I'm honest with my feedback, unlike some lecturers, pouring honey on everything."

Mark Rowe was one of these; he would dip them in sugar by the ankles just to look up their skirts. Mark had recently been promoted to senior lecturer at the university and was using his position to his advantage.

Martha tidied her face in her compact and said she

wanted to get out of here; she didn't like not looking her best in public. She suggested we go to hers and continue working, excusing her shoddy plot line on recently being dumped and promising a nice bottle of red on arrival. I went along with it, after all I enjoy the way they hang on my every word. I was now feeling better than I had for some time.

Grabbing two glasses and a bottle of supermarket wine, Martha prompted me to sit down on the sofa next to her.

"Wine and music always spark my creative side," she said.

I nodded in agreement as she leaned over me to turn on the radio. Bad Moon Rising aired out and I smiled, suggesting Martha watch some Polanski films. She took out her phone, I assume to research my advice. I let myself sink back into the chair and fell into the music. My peace, almost perfect, was soon broken when I heard the soft lilting tones of the presenter's voice, a voice I hadn't heard in almost a year, but a voice I could not mistake. The air in the room changed; my mind closed in. It was Sally's voice. I stood up, my heart pounding like a tribal drum. I looked round the flat, but it wasn't Martha's flat anymore, it was Sally's. I saw us both sitting there, Sally gently holding my hand and telling me how we could never be, never were. She was rejecting me all over again.

"Today is not the day."

I twitched and looked up; it was Martha, fucking Martha.

"What?" I cried.

"I said is everything okay?" She handed me a glass of red, which I quickly drained and made an excuse to leave. Martha hovered in the doorway as I took off into the night.

Turning my collar to the wind, my mind was racing as I walked the wide empty high street. How could Sally sink so low, a beautiful girl, so sharp witted, so full of promise, full of ideas, now working as a jibber jabber at Radio Tees, the headquarters of the banal and the bland. It wasn't so long ago we were together, discussing her ideas and her bright future, our bright future. I couldn't stand the idea of her being reduced to a common entertainer. Sally, the girl who would stay up all night discussing Hemingway and Orwell, politics and poetry, poetry for God's sake! How hard it had been to find a woman with a keen ear in this town. We would poke fun at the other students in my class, the Big Brother viewers and the Tarantino wannabes. She was my brightest by far, drafting melodramas of people escaping war torn countries. She listened to my lectures, researched the topics and questioned the facts. How could she degrade herself like this: parroting the text messages of morons and dishing up the latest celebrity gossip. It was more than I could bear. I marched by the river, pausing to watch the swirling ebbs below, seeing myself as a distorted reflection in the gloomy depths. I thought of Sally and how she had returned into my life. Today will not be the day.

The next morning I was at the university, head down and feeling ill tempered through lack of sleep. I cut through the conviviality like a shark through shoaling fish. I knew I had to reach her again. I always wondered whether she really meant her rejection or it was more a knee jerk reaction she had developed; someone that strong willed would have trouble letting anyone else in. Maybe she just needed more convincing evidence. I was nearing the lecture hall when I was cut short by a tall figure in front of me. It was Mark. Mark had recently taken to wearing a beige corduroy blazer adorned with leather elbow patches; I assume he thought he looked the part. He was looking at me solemnly and I could see he had something to tell. I stared at him blankly waiting for him to speak.

Several long moments passed before he began.

"We've been told to streamline the department, mate. With media studies losing favour and more people enrolling in STEM subjects, I guess we're becoming old news… there's a fair amount of pressure on us if we're going to survive at all. Now you know I think highly of the work you do round here and you've the knowledge and experience we need but I'm hearing a lot of talk about your extra curricular activities… You know as well as anyone I'm in favour of the one to one approach but it may be misconstrued as giving particular attention to one or two students above the others and that won't look good to the Board. They'll be talking with all members of the department to see how best to handle it, just a friendly heads up… If you want my advice, you should try and find a girl outside this place for a change. I've found a proper stunner over at Broadcasting house, that lass from the evening show no less. A local celebrity, anyway, it's something to think about... We'll be in touch."

With that Mark drifted into the middle distance. I turned and retraced my steps home. I had to make contact with Sally. If I could rekindle the affection we felt for each other and she realised my intentions were true, there would still be a chance for us.

Back at the flat I ransacked my papers and shelves, cupboards and cases searching for some sincere scrap of evidence. There must be something here of our time together, some nugget in the mud. I up-turned my desk drawer and there, facing up at me from the floor, as if by grace, was exactly the thing I was looking for: a poem I'd penned especially for her. I picked it up and examined it. It was all there, the version I'd sent: 'The Brightest Star In My Darkest Night'. I remember how she enjoyed the title and expressed her love of romantic poetry while likening it to Keats. I heard the birds sing outside. This was the answer, this would put the pieces of her and I back together. This was what she'd been looking for, a true love, not the smooth talk and elbow patches of Rowe but the real thing. Surely she had realised what he was. He could never connect with her on that level, our level, I mean for God's sake, he was a brute. What did he mean by threatening my job and thrusting their love in my face? He would soon learn.

But how to get the poem to her without coming on too strong? I still had her number, but calling her up would be too sober, and bumping into her in the street could prove problematic where romance was concerned. My eyes drifted around the room, gliding across the wild array of papers and books until I spied the old valve radio in the corner. Of course, the radio. I would send it to her whilst she was on air. Perhaps she would read it whilst sitting there at her little desk and remember me. She would recognise the poem and remember what we had and how we were meant to be. Perhaps she would read it aloud to the whole of Teesside and say my name, ask me to meet her, imploring me to come to the studio for critical acclaim and kisses, declaring her love for all to hear.

I quickly began drafting the poem as an email, savouring every word, as Sally would when she read it again. In no time at all it was there in front of me in all its backlit glory and I marvelled. This was the proof she needed to open her heart to me, to be free.

Before hitting send, I changed one detail. I removed my name and left a single kiss at the bottom. There was no doubt she would know what this was, an open letter to her heart. I clicked the magic key and sat back pleased, only a matter of time now and all the pieces would come together. My ruminations were soon jarred by a knock at the door. I pulled myself up, straightened myself out and answered. It was Martha. She looked perplexed and peered straight through me, examining my flat with a furrowed brow.

"What's going on?" she enquired. "You weren't there for your lecture today and now all this mess? Is everything okay?"

"Sure," I replied coolly. "I'm just redecorating."

"But everything's upside down. You look… well, out of sorts, I'd say. I better come in." She pushed her way past me and examined the flat further.

"I'm just redecorating. Honestly, there's no problem. I couldn't make the lecture as I was waiting for the paint to dry."

Obviously this was going to be a hard sell.

Martha sat down on the desk chair and took my hand, looking up at me with her big wet eyes. I could see she was putting words together in her mind.

"You're such an intelligent soul… you have so much to offer and you dedicate so much time to me and my problems even though I know a lot of it probably seems trivial to you."

"It's quite alright, no need to thank me. It's my job and well, now's not really the time." Sally's show was starting soon and I didn't want to miss a beat, but Martha pushed on.

"It's more than that and you know it. You're not employed to meet me by the fire every other evening. You know what I think? I think what you really need is a good woman by your side." She wasn't wrong there, but then again she was way off the mark. She squeezed my hand tentatively. "…and what I came here to say was I want to be that woman."

She stood up with an awkward shuffle and took my other hand as well. She was like an officer about to take down a suspect. I stepped back and stumbled on some of the debris.

"I know you have a hard time letting anyone in, and I'm here to tell you I understand." She moved her face towards mine, her lips puckered.

Was this woman mad? Did she not realise I belonged to another?

"Martha," I said, "this is all very well but you must realise I'm with someone."

"Don't be coy. I know there's no woman in your life, not unless you count those air-heads in class."

Who did this harlot think she was? I felt the room spin.

"Martha, you've got to leave now. This isn't what I want, Martha."

"You never know what you want." She slid her hand toward my groin like some sort of she-beast and in the clumsy assault we toppled backward over my briefcase.

"Look what you've done now, you slut!" I boomed. "You're ruining this for me and Sally!"

I dragged her onto her feet and threw her out the door, her head ricocheting against the jamb on exit. I just glimpsed the twisted expression on her face before slamming the door on it.

I busied myself cleaning up the shamble of notes and papers, waiting for Sally's evening show to start. At seven o'clock I switched on the radio to a myriad of thuds and jingles before Sally's voice broke the racket. After an hour or so of music and gossip made tolerable only by her gentle voice she announced she would be reading out readers' messages. Electricity rippled through my spine. A letter regarding stolen wheely bins was discussed amid chuckles before she got to the poem.

"And now we have a special treat for you all, an anonymous listener has sent me a self-penned poem and I'd like to read it to you."

I could barely contain myself.

A slight pause for dramatic effect then: "The Brightest Star In My Darkest Night," then from nowhere the Benny Hill theme tune rang out and Sally delivered the golden lines I'd gifted her as a comic farce, giggling intermittently. After the reading she caught her breath. "I don't know what you've been drinking, whoever you are, but I want some!"

How could Sally do this to us? Did she not recognise the poem, the meaning, the evidence? I could stomach no more. I snatched the radio plug from its socket, grabbed my phone and dug out Sally's number, sending another anonymous message. This time I asked her to meet me in the high street after the show, signing the message Mark. I made my way to Victoria Bridge, knowing she'd have to cross it to meet Mark.

I loitered on the bridge, walking this way and that so as to look natural when Sally approached. It wasn't long before her slender figure caught my eye; there was no mistaking that gentle walk with its measured steps. Head down, I walked towards her, hoping she would recognise me. She walked straight by me so I made the first move.

"Sally?"

She was startled and I came closer to be heard over the wind. "Sally, is that you?"

"Yes, who's that?"

"It's me, Sally, don't you see?" I pushed my hair to one side and straightened my jacket.

"Oh, yes, of course… How are you? It's been a while."

"I'm good, thanks. I heard your show tonight."

"Oh, yeah, what did you think?"

"I was interested to hear the poem."

She giggled. "Oh yes, we get a lot of that sort of thing, these loons send in any half-baked idea hoping for air play. I read it out to discourage them. You get it, don't you?"

I moved closer to embrace her but she backed away, so I settled for her hand and took it in mine.

"Sally, don't you see? We can be together now. All the pieces are in place."

I wrapped my arms tightly around her and felt her warm embrace.

"I'll never let go, Sall. Here is the proof, today is the day."

I moved us towards the rail and let our momentum carry us over the edge, feeling the cold air brush against us. I let out an aching sigh of relief to finally have her.

MAGGIE
JANE BRADLEY

Of course, I'm not in the photographs – the ones that were plastered ostentatiously over the front page of every newspaper in the country the next morning. I never expected to be.

But I was there that day – right by her side – and that is what matters.

I almost didn't make it in time – due, of course, to matters entirely outside of my control.

I had informed my boss that I had a dentist appointment to attend that afternoon. This was a falsehood, of course, but I had decided that a small white lie wouldn't hurt on this most special of days. This minor untruth had secured me permission to leave ninety minutes before my usual time of departure, which would, I had calculated, give me exactly an hour to travel to my destination.

I had set myself a carefully timetabled schedule of

work for the day to ensure my early exit, when, out of nowhere, he dropped a pile of papers on my desk: a stack of files, dozens of letters to type.

He'd sauntered off to the site in his ludicrous hard hat and safety boots, blowing me a kiss through his blubbery lips as he left, a smirk spreading over his face. I looked away in disgust.

However, I had no choice. I began to work like a whirling dervish. I had to finish my duties, as unfairly assigned as they were, as swiftly as possible. I had to see her.

My typewriter keys were humming as I efficiently and rapidly worked my way through the papers. I could feel the other girls' eyes on me. A smile touched my lips. I might be decades older than them, but I am still far quicker.

Then, just as I was preparing to leave, performing a last minute touch up to my coiffure, scrabbling around for my bus fare in the bottom of my handbag, the wail of the sirens began.

For a minute, I considered making a run for it, dashing across the acrid car park in my low heeled courts as the stench of whatever chemical they'd let leak out today began to fill the air, but I knew if the boss caught me, I would be starkly reprimanded.

The other secretaries were aimlessly wandering about, slowly closing any open windows as if they had all of the time in the world. There were a lot of windows to close, it was a warm day for September.

I went to open the door to the boss's office. I knew

he would have opted for a breath of fresh air today – his cheap polyester shirt had already been saturated with sweat as he'd stood over my desk that morning – but Patricia jumped forward to stop me as my fingers touched the handle, her frosted perm bobbing self importantly.

"Oi! You cannut go in THERE! It's private."

I opened my mouth to remonstrate with her, but shut it again.

It was typical of Patricia, wanting to keep the boss's private space private, even in a toxic emergency. The windows are wide open, the chemical particles are seeping in. But we can't go in there to seal the building, it's against the rules. Let us all be killed because Patricia's minute brain cannot separate guidelines from common sense. Loathsome woman.

I sat back down at my desk, trying not to picture the tiny particles of toxic seepage floating in on the air drifting through the wide open space. I held my breath. I noticed Patricia watching me through her little piggy eyes. She'd tried to make them look bigger by drawing a line of bright blue pencil around them, but she just looked ridiculous, like all of the young women today.

When I'd met HER of course, she had looked perfect. Immaculately set hair. Understated makeup. Like a lady should look.

It was almost forty years ago now, I calculated. It had been 1948 when we first met. But her look was timeless.

I reopened the mirror on my Elizabeth Arden compact

and checked my light pink lipstick again. Adequate, I thought. For my age.

The hands on my watch were moving fast, too fast. My heart was pounding under my cream, faux silk blouse. I hoped fervently that I would be able to leave soon.

When she'd come into the office the first time, it had been the head of the secretarial department who had told me to look after her.

It was a big responsibility, she told me, one that she wouldn't usually grant to someone of my tender years. I had been thrilled.

Of course, she was no one then, not to most people.

She had looked right at me. She even said my name.

"Jean," she'd trilled, in that high, fluty voice. She twisted her mouth into a toothy smile, the one I now know so well. "Jean, could you possibly get me a cup of tea? My mouth is SO dry."

I still have the teacup with her lipstick mark on it. The saucer too. I'd shoved them into my bag after she left the room. I didn't know why at the time, I just knew they were important to keep, but I'm glad I did now.

I display them now in pride of place in my house, on the top shelf of my corner cabinet. I can't risk them being knocked to the ground by one of the cats, so I have attached them to the shelf with Superglue. It is quite an acceptable solution.

She wasn't like most people who apply for jobs here. She was female, to begin with. She was the first lady chemist I'd ever seen, not that I've come across many since.

Of course, some of my co-workers were horrified.

"A woman?" they'd scoffed. "She won't last two minutes in here."

And she didn't. She never got a chance to show them how wonderful she was, how talented. How masterful.

They rejected her out of hand. I know, because I kept my eye on her file, in the depths of the personnel basement, where I became accustomed to spending my tea breaks.

The file described her as "headstrong, obstinate and dangerously self-opinionated". Bigots. She was none of those things, I knew that.

I kept checking that file, hoping I'd missed something, that they'd say they made a mistake, that the rejection letter they'd sent her on the day she had been interviewed had been issued erroneously. I hoped that one day I would walk into the office and there she would be, sitting at one of the senior management desks, wearing that dark blue suit.

Of course, that never happened.

For a while, I considered applying for a job at a plastics company in Essex, where, according to the Curriculum Vitae she'd submitted to personnel, she had worked at the time. Her initials were printed on the top of every single page of the resume: MR. I admired her attention to detail.

However, by the time I filled out the application form, she'd left, moved on to bigger and better things. It is a shame. We would have been a great team, she and I.

I was awoken from my reverie by the sound of giggling.

It was Patricia again, staring at me through those tiny eye sockets. I wondered, briefly, as I often do, how she ever manages to see anything clearly.

"What are you thinking about, Jeanie?" she asked, poking her friend – another moron in blue eyeshadow who sits next to her – firmly in the ribs.

"You must be in love!"

I scowled at her. I hate being called Jeanie, always have, ever since I was a child. Common-sounding name. Unbecoming.

Before I could reply, the siren sounded again. The all clear. Finally.

I quickly but carefully arranged my handbag on my arm, picked up my umbrella and walked out of the door without a word.

To my great fortune, a bus was waiting at the bottom of the road. I alighted and paid my fare before settling impatiently into my seat. Half past two, the news had said. I checked my watch. It was 2.14pm. I felt unsettled. It is not like me to be tardy.

The bus turned onto the bridge. And then stopped. There was a queue of traffic in front of us. I hadn't realised so many people would want to see her. Ridiculous, of course, who wouldn't want to see her?

The Tees stretched out below me, a gulf between me and her – she was so close I could almost touch her, just there, on the other side of the water.

I cross the bridge every day to attend work. Now, for the first time, I was looking at it through her eyes.

What did she think of the grey, expansive water stretching between two patches of scrubland? What could she possibly have to say?

Finally, the cars began to move and to my huge relief, the bus made it to the other side of the bridge. 2.23pm.

It was not a bus stop I would commonly use these days, I felt quite strange getting off there.

There is nothing nearby, just a wasteland where a factory once stood. I had worked there briefly in the 1970s, but the standard of typing among the secretarial staff had not been as high as at my usual place of employment, so it was but a year before I returned.

As I walked east along the river, I could see the shabby buildings of Stockton town centre rising up in the distance.

There were policemen everywhere. I must be in the right place, I thought. I marched up to one of them and tugged at his sleeve.

"Pardon me, sir," I attempted, using my most assertive voice, the one I muster when Patricia is behaving at her worst. "You have to let me through. I am an old friend of the lady over there."

He barely looked at me. "Behind the line, Madam," he muttered.

I stepped back.

A gentleman next to me was beginning to become agitated, waving a thick pile of papers he carried under his arm. He wore a thick donkey jacket and I wondered why he did not feel the heat.

To my consternation, he started to shout and curse.

"F-ing Tories," he bellowed. "Three million unemployed! What are you going to do for us? One thousand rejection letters I've got here."

Then, suddenly, there she was. Striding across the wasteland, the grey expanse of the Tees looming behind her.

Despite the cluster of security guards, policemen, assorted press photographers and gawping members of the public standing just feet away, she looked alone, so alone. But magnificent.

I wanted to tell her that she didn't need to be alone, that I would always be there for her, to serve in whatever way she needed me to.

I pushed the swearing man aside and ducked under the police cordon.

"Miss Roberts!" I shouted, tottering towards her, my modest heels slipping on the dusty ground. I noticed we were both clutching our near-identical red handbags tightly to our sides.

"Miss Roberts! It's me, Jean."

The Prime Minister's eyes met mine for a second before her security guards surrounded her.

I am certain she knew me.

After all, I have not changed dramatically since our initial meeting.

I know she definitely hasn't.

THE SHOPKEEPER
SUE CAMPBELL

The shop was one of a row of well-kept, bow-windowed businesses on the main street. Fresh white paint adorned the outside woodwork, announcing its name on the facia board – Jennings Jewellers, Middlesbrough – in a shiny Cooper Black typeface.

Gordon Jennings – son of the original Mr Jennings, who had opened the shop in 1914 – was keen on a nice typeface. They fascinated him – the stories behind them, the shapes, the styles, the fonts. He liked modern typefaces – it was 1964 after all. He'd tried Anarko and even Jimi, but had settled on the more solid and dependable Cooper Black. It looked much more permanent, reassuring. He'd toyed with colours – carmine red, Oxford blue, sage green. But none had the character of a glossy black.

Gordon's entrepreneurial father had founded the shop at the start of the First World War. He'd later shipped over to France with the Durham Light Infantry and got himself killed along with thousands of compatriots in the mud and the mire at the Somme in 1916. Gordon had been born nine months after his father's last leave earlier that year, so had nothing of him to remember. He gleaned little from his mother, Elsa, who always seemed cross with his father when she talked about him, which was hardly at all. It was if he had left them deliberately and unforgivably.

All that was left of his father for Gordon were a few dog-eared sepia photographs of a short, stocky man with a flourishing blond moustache. Gordon supposed he should miss him, but he couldn't miss what he never had and his father remained just a grainy picture in a silver frame that bore his name – Reginald Hubert Jennings – in a charming Bodoni Italic. Gordon kept it in the living room in his flat above the shop, which was, after all, his legacy.

Elsa had kept the shop going, with help of part-time assistants, until Gordon gradually took over. By age twelve he was expertly selecting stock, pricing up and serving customers. His devotion to the shop meant he made few real friends. While they were playing football, scrumping apples or playing on the Slaggy Island coal heaps, he was learning about gemstones and window dressing.

Gordon had a somewhat distant relationship with his mother, who had been fine-boned, slim – even beautiful – when young, but seemed to fold in on herself and fade to thin and sallow as she aged. She always seemed vaguely disappointed with how things had turned out. She'd crossed the Tees, from Seaton Carew to Middlesbrough to marry Reginald and seemed to spend the rest of her life regretting it. Nothing seemed to match up to her expectations. If Gordon had articulated it, he would have said that included both himself and the long dead Reginald.

Elsa died of a stroke in 1934. He had gone to deliver her early morning cup of tea – "strong enough to stand a spoon in," she always demanded, no sugar and a splash of milk. Gordon had found her laid out on her bedroom floor. Her eyes glassy, one arm stretched out towards the door with the hand curled as if beckoning. She was still in her day clothes from the evening before and was quite, quite cold. Gordon had looked at her for a while, drinking the dark, pungent tea, and thinking he'd never have to make that bitter brew again.

The funeral was a strangely unemotional event. It wasn't that he didn't love his mother, or she him, but it had been a dutiful love, unencumbered by comfort or joy. Gordon had the funeral service printed in eye-catching Helvetica Bold and had the service at St Peter's in South Bank, his mother being what he thought of as an occasional Catholic, followed by tea for the dozen or so people who attended back in the flat.

When he closed the door on the last of the neighbours, one distant cousin from Darlington, the priest and a couple of gem suppliers from Newcastle, he felt a sense of relief and finality. A door firmly closing.

Gordon supposed he could have made a break then. Left Middlesbrough and seen the world. Swapped traversing the Tees for spanning the Amazon. Travelled the British Isles and beyond, had adventures, seen the pyramids, the Grand Canyon, the Eiffel Tower. Blackpool Tower even. He thought about it for a long time, even picked up some colourful brochures from the travel agents. But somehow, the months slipped away, the shop enveloped him and became his life, his beloved typefaces his outlet. The dust settled on the brochures on the coffee table. And Gordon just, well, settled.

The few who knew him thought it was a shame that Gordon never married. He wasn't bad looking – a bit taller than his father, and with his father's blondness. He'd tried once to grow a thick moustache like Reginald's, but rather than luxurious, it had come in sparse and mousey. It just didn't take.

Gordon had stepped out a few times in his twenties with a girl from Stockton called Myrtle, who had come into the shop to get a bracelet repaired. There was a bit of mild flirting on her part and Gordon surprised himself by asking her out to tea. Myrtle had dark curly hair, a high pitched laugh and a slight wall-eye. But it turned out Myrtle liked Latin dancing and craved passion, whereas Gordon liked a good book and craved a quiet life. That didn't take either.

A year later he'd seen in the local paper the notice – in pleasing Times New Roman in a box with a fancy border – of Myrtle's engagement to a man called Frank from

Grangetown. Gordon hoped Frank could at least tango, for Myrtle's sake. And Frank's own.

Gordon hadn't served in the war – being a jeweller was hardly a reserved occupation, but flat feet and mild asthma put paid to any military ambitions. So his life became a comfortable routine. Never a small man, he put on weight and indulged his sweet tooth with cakes and toffees.

Gordon didn't hold with holidays. The odd day out at Albert Park or Ormesby Hall was his idea of a good break, and the only money he spent unsparingly was on books and artefacts concerning fonts and typography, the history of printers and type founders from Gutenberg to Bruce Rogers. He built up a significant collection, which he displayed on shelves in his big square living room, and he made himself quite an authority. But the pleasure of knowing and the beauty of his belongings were confined to his quiet flat.

Business was steady, the people of Middlesbrough were loyal customers and regularly got engaged and married, had birthdays, anniversaries and retirements and returned over again to his well kept shop, which always smelled of furniture polish and lavender.

The only fly in Gordon's ointment was the construction three years previously of 'the precinct', an ugly word which described the architecturally worthless pedestrianised cluster of shops at the top of the street. It housed cheap stores, bookmakers and an inferior branch of a chain of jewellers. No competition to Gordon's fine stock, but still…

It had also brought what Gordon thought of as louts. Raucous groups of teenagers, usually boys, who haunted the precinct and got into mischief, tipping over displays, swearing loudly and leaving empty cider bottles and chip wrappers next to – but never in – the unpleasant looking and malodorous circular concrete bins.

One or two older ones, the ringleaders, clearly feckless and jobless, encouraged the younger ones to greater disruption and petty theft, stealing apples from outside the greengrocers, nicking pop from the little shop and magazines from the newsagents. Gordon watched them from his window, shouting the odds and intimidating passersby. He'd rung the police several times to complain. They turned up occasionally and moved the gangs on, but the louts simply returned when the police were out of sight.

When their younger followers weren't around – likely at school or bunking off somewhere else – the older lads paraded up and down the more established part of the street. They made a habit of peering in windows, opening doors, knocking over stands, laughing and swearing and shouting obscene remarks at young women, who scurried past them in alarm.

Just that morning, in a quiet moment, Gordon had gazed out of the shop window, and was startled to find one of the louts staring back at him. White faced, greasy haired with a cigarette hanging from his lips, he smiled faintly. He wasn't looking at the artfully displayed engagement and wedding rings in Gordon's well-lit, tastefully dressed window. He was looking at Gordon. Straight at Gordon. Gordon felt a frisson of fear, but had stared back until the lout had broken eye contact, turned and sauntered off.

Maybe he'd call the police again, he pondered. No, perhaps not – there wasn't very much to report was there? The lout hadn't done anything but look in his window – hardly a crime. Gordon tried to dismiss the incident from his mind, but it lingered.

It had been a slowish morning in the shop. Gordon polished the glass-topped wood-framed cabinets until they gleamed, and swept the contents with a feather duster until they sparkled.

He'd served one man who wanted the diamond ring of his obviously significantly sized late grandmother made smaller to fit the hand of his new slimmer fiancée. He'd replaced a couple of watch straps, taken a gold bracelet in for cleaning and a set of pearls for re-stringing. One of his suppliers dropped in briefly for a chat, and the woman from the gown shop next door popped her head in to ask him to take a delivery of dresses for her that afternoon, as she was attending a fitting in Guisborough.

He closed as usual at noon for half an hour, turning the notice suspended on the door that told customers when he'd return. There was just time for a tinned salmon sandwich – Gordon was particularly fond of tinned salmon, soused in malt vinegar and sprinkled with pepper. It was accompanied by a cup of tea and a cream cake that he purchased daily from the baker's two doors up – today it was a chocolate éclair – and a glance through the local daily paper.

He liked his local paper, and especially the rather unusual Octin Vintage typeface they used for the headlines, which he found pleasing to the eye. It was good to keep in touch with local news, and what was going on in the rest of the world. One of the stories was about the death of Harpo Marx, which saddened him a little. He rather liked the Marx Brothers' brand of humour and he related somewhat to the silent Harpo.

At 12.30pm sharp he descended, turned round the notice and unlocked the shop door. He'd hardly turned round when he was shoved mightily in the small of the back and he lurched forward, arms flailing. He'd have fallen flat if he hadn't landed, sizeable stomach first, against a display cabinet, rattling the glass and knocking the wind out of him.

He gasped for breath, red faced, and turned slowly to find the lout from the staring match that morning, locking the door. He was no more pleasant-looking than he'd been earlier and had a thin sheen of sweat on his cheeks. He might have been in his early twenties, but he had the look of someone older and used to the streets.

"Where's the cash?" Local accent, abrasive and demanding.

"Cash?" croaked Gordon, stunned.

"Yes, money, you old get. I know you're wadded. Now give!" The lout brought his right hand out of his pocket. In his thin fingers was a wicked-looking blade, about four inches long, which flashed and gleamed under the shop lights.

Gordon looked at it and then at him. Surprise gave way to anger, which pulsed through him. He stared at this youth, this thief, this stranger, this lout in his shop.

In a few seconds, Gordon calmly considered his options. Gordon's whole life had been uneventful, dull, predictable. He could let the lout have what he wanted. He'd got plenty of money in the bank – what did he spend it on? There was only about £20 in the till – he banked every day – so there was never much on the premises. Gordon would hardly miss it. It would make the news. The headline in the local paper would read something like 'Shopkeeper Robbed at Knifepoint', probably on page seven or nine, maybe in News Gothic type.

But what if he didn't hand the cash over? What if he refused the lout and threw him out? He'd be a kind of local hero. Someone of some stature, someone people would talk about, even look up to. Someone his father might have been proud of. He'd be a minor celebrity for a time. He could see the headline now – 'Shopkeeper Overpowers Robber'. Now that might make page two or three.

Gordon made his mind up. "No," he said firmly.

The lout looked dumbfounded, his eyebrows raised in astonishment. "No?"

"No," said Gordon again. He rose to his full height and started to shift his considerable weight purposefully towards the startled youth.

The lout's eyes suddenly filled with panic at this unexpected turn of events. He'd thought this was going to be easy – in and out in two minutes with a wodge of cash. He hadn't planned on heroics from this fat, slow shopkeeper. He made to turn, bravado leaking away, scrabbling at the door to unlock it. But Gordon was on him, adrenaline coursing through his veins, pinning the lout's arms to his sides.

They struggled for a moment, the lout squealing for Gordon to let go, but he held on tight. Then, all at once, Gordon felt a strange sensation. A cold, searing pain in his chest, sudden and surprising and sharp. And then down his arm, both a numbness and a tingling.

Oh God, the knife – it must be the knife. But no. As he slid bonelessly to the ground, he saw the lout still had the blade, clean of blood, in his now shaking hand.

Gordon lay half propped against a display case. It was as if a vice were being tightened slowly round his ribcage, his breath being squeezed from him, his lungs unable to draw.

The lout loomed over him, eyes wide. Then he turned, fumbled with the lock, crashed open the door so hard it rattled on its hinges, and fled. Gordon lay there, listening to the lout's receding footsteps and the shouts of passersby as he cannoned off them.

Gordon's world was going grey at the edges, the lights dimming, air wheezing from his lungs, his heart hiccupping and slowing. Too many cream cakes, too many toffees, too many sedentary hours in the armchair, looking at his typography books, turning over his treasures in his pudgy hands.

Gordon closed his eyes for the last time and a small smile played on his lips, even as his breath finally sighed away.

He reckoned he'd make the headlines after all, maybe even the nationals. 'Shopkeeper Dies in Failed Robbery'. Maybe even page one. Bodoni Bold would be nice.

RESTORATION RIVER
RACHEL CAMSELL

A peach-sun descended impressively across the Tees, the pear-green grass basked beneath it. Children paddled, families picnicked, intellects read, elderly reflected. In the epicentre of post-war and summer liberation, he stood, incongruous to those who were unacquainted with the revulsive and deplorable abilities of humankind and attempted to find his way. He limped down the riverbank, self-consciously, hoping no one would detect the disturbed, deprived, pitiable person he had become. A far cry from the sanguine and strong man he was six years prior.

Hobbling down the bank, he became captivated by a vision of beauty and promise. Elegantly, she kneeled on the crispy grass, barefoot, wearing a meadow-print ivory tea dress, and her hair was plaited like a thornless rosebush. Across her lap lay a daisy chain; her gentle hands were waxy from piercing through multiple stems. This was the beginning of a cataclysm of feelings that remained strong over half a century later. He noticed the supressed eagerness which danced across her expression as she beckoned him over, creating a wave – a ripple of high tide's falling water – a swell under his chest, deep beneath the gunshot wound.

Fervent but fretful, he crossed the stout-coloured stream on the river bank. Dark-haired, dark-eyed, mysterious yet uncomplicated, she read his story from his face. Loneliness in him and the peculiarity of this place held his tongue tight. Peace, tranquillity and serenity were foreign to him. His bruised mind was a chamber of horror: smothered and suffocated by incessant sounds of bullets spiralling through the air and the inevitable crimson mess which always lingered afterwards. Even after it ended, ceaseless visions of human evil and unnecessary annihilation replayed in his mind. In time, the show would wane, the curtain would fall – just like her chain.

Overwhelmed by her cordiality, he was obliged to accept the berries she had picked on her way to the river and to share with her cheese, crusty bread and wine. She spoke of art, family and the land skills she'd acquired. He nodded and gazed, intrigued by normality and winced as his vision was blocked by bursts of bloody brutality.

Recognising a need to change scenery, they crossed the river, barefoot, and advanced upstream. The water, still motionless despite the succession of water, flew like bullets and collected in a foamy messy heap from High Force not far away. A dislodged rock made him stumble and forced him to recall a struggle – one of the worst attacks. Anamnesis was sepsis of the mind and he would experience it often, penetrating his thoughts, visions, senses. It was on this day when he began to fight back against the anguish. The river was his antidote.

He hoisted himself to safety on to the riverbank, falling in a heap. A scar on his left knee was exposed. Behind it, buried a seed of shrapnel, a sinister souvenir from the foreign land. With delicate carnation-like fingers she traced the mark.

With the encounter, seeds of hope began to bud between the pavement cracks further up the bank. Happiness gleaned off the murky water. Optimism echoed in the sounds of laughter and human interactions. The encounter at the river became his crutch, his reason to move on.

Above them, clouds of birds coalesced and scattered to constellations on hills which dimmed the brightening of the ground. The summer night was closing, the moon began to flow through the leaves above between the trees. The air ran cool. They sat, cross-legged on a fallen tree trunk, laughing, talking, and not being downbeat by the constraints of conflict. Around them, leaves fell like confetti.

Though his descendants never knew of his painful past, he visited the harmonious haven habitually:

Fifty years ago he initiated his commitment to her.

Forty years ago he paddled and picnicked with his children.

Thirty years ago he captured his place on a blank canvas with watercolours.

Twenty years ago he introduced the next generation to her.

Ten years ago he felt obliged to payback and planted a bed of daffodils.

On his final visit, there was a disparity in the landscape to which he had become well accustomed. For the first time ever, the sunlight was a beam of silvery light, burning and sparkling as though it emanated the promise of freedom forever. The small fragments of his face which were still frozen from emotion-paralysis, melted and his mood bubbled like the foaming base of High Force which splashed, alive and glittering in the twilight in the near distance. Taking it all in, his lungs inflated with the onrush of the ineffable scenery: air, water, grass, trees… liberation.

"It's time," an anonymous whisper sounded to his right.

He was ready. Paid back.

Then, the last of the pain withered like stars at dawn. It vanished. The guns. Bullets. Bombs. Tanks. Enemy. Scars. Blood. Bruises. Tears. Screams. Cries. Pain.

It was gone.

Along with the ashes and the dust, he drifted across peaceful pastures, immersed and forever rested in the sequestered serenity of the valley, his saviour, his home, his place.

THE BRIDGE
ARTHUR DUNCAN

The bridge stood there, as it always had done, and for as long as anyone could remember. No one knew who built it, or when, or why. No path or road led to or from it, no foot had trod its span, no animal or bird came near. Its stones were thick with moss, its feet straddled the River Teise, the Teise that whispered and chuckled its way down under the bridge, then ran and leapt towards the sea.

There was no reason for it to be there, but it was there, sitting, cradled between the steep scars of the dale, waiting, waiting as it always had done, and for a time so far past that even Time itself had forgotten it was there.

Above the dale, storm clouds gathered. The gently falling rain gathered momentum, lightning flashed, thunder hammered and echoed between the scars, loosening soil and rock. A blistering streak shattered a huge rock sitting proud on a flat seat. The rain pounded on, washing away the pieces. Lightning revealed a large sarcophagus resting within the rock.

Inside, something stirred, it was awake, the noise and movement had disturbed the creature from a deep sleep. The rain, dripping through a crack in the lid, was enough to revive an Elven Warrior Queen, and, with some effort, she forced the lid apart. Her heart was full of hatred and lusted for revenge, revenge against the Evil Ones that had imprisoned her.

She stood naked in the rain, allowing the water to wash off aeons of dirt and waste, cleansing her body; she was pure again. Removing her clothing from within the sarcophagus, she dressed; it would give her some protection against this rain and cold.

Gathering up her weapons and strapping them to her body, Rosalyne, the Queen of all Elven Warriors, was ready for battle against Evil; as she finished, the setting sun burst through the clouds sending rays of golden light into the dale, illuminating the Queen and the Bridge.

Her feet carried her onto the Bridge; cautiously she took a step, then another, and another, and a strange new world unfolded, a world so different to that from which she had come. The Bridge whispered to her, "Go forth, my Queen, you have a task to fulfil," then it closed the portal to her lands. It would remain closed until the Queen had avenged the wrong that had been done to her, her people, and her world.

Looking round, she knew nothing of this new world, a world of green, a world of living things, not unlike her old world, the world Evil had destroyed with ignorance, greed and corruption. That world had become sterile, hot, dry, barren, and nothing grew. She could not understand what had happened here. Walking lightly over this green carpet, the warrior marvelled at the life within its cover and carried on. Darkness was falling, and not being familiar with this land, she found shelter and slept.

A rain-swept dawn crept up and gently woke her, fruit and berries helped fend off the hunger she was feeling, and finding dry material, she lit a fire that would warm and dry her; she would venture forth when the rain ceased.

The late afternoon sun brought warmth and the Warrior Queen continued in safety, finally emerging in the pastures at the foot of the dale. Strange beasts walked across this land. She avoided them. Dwellings appeared, and the warrior within her approached with caution. She sensed Evil. Creeping forward, she saw them, Mortals, evil and armed, attacking an older unarmed mortal. With eyes full of hate, she rushed forward and pushed the older one to the ground, her swords flashed in anger; the Evil Ones would not fight again. Another, waiting in a strange chariot... her knife blade was silent and deadly in its work. Though revenge was sweet, she did not recognise the strange things here in this land and moved on.

Soon, the warrior within her was tiring. This being her first venture into this strange world, she needed to find food and shelter for the night.

The Dales Café lay at the edge of the large village. Ken, the new owner, had finished cleaning up and was sitting drinking coffee when he became aware of a dark figure outlined on the glass door. Not being the type to turn potential customers away, he went over, opened the door, stood back and gestured to the figure to enter.

Rosalyne, hand on sword, warily entered this place and looked round. This mortal, was not of the Evil Ones, and it was trying to communicate with her, but she could not understand.

"Would my lady care to eat?" said Ken.

She was well over six foot and though her cloak and hood covered her body, plenty of weapons were visible and, thinking she had been involved with the village fayre and was still play acting, he decided to go along with this charade.

She did not answer, but continued to look round; it was all strange to her.

Ken guided her to a table.

Looking again at this mortal, she felt safe and placed her weapons on the floor and table.

"How about some soup?" he said, fetching a bowl of soup with buttered bread rolls, and placed it in front of her. This free offer had proved successful before in attracting new customers. "Try that." He handed her a spoon, then on hearing sirens, turned towards the door.

The Queen looked at the spoon. It was familiar, something triggered her actions and she started to eat.

Outside, police cars with blue lights and sirens screamed past. "I wonder where that lot are going?" he remarked.

Ken came back over, stood in front of the girl and looked at the weapons.

Whoever made those weapons was very good, he thought, and tried to pick up the sword. It was incredibly heavy. He examined the workmanship whilst the girl continued to eat and observe him...

"If you want to wait, I'll cook something and we can eat together; I haven't had anything to eat yet." Ken moved to the kitchen area and started preparing left over chicken.

With the meal ready, he gestured to the girl to put all the weapons on another table out of the way and brought the plates over. With a glass of apple juice each, they commenced eating the meal. Up to now the girl hadn't spoken; Ken wondered if she was foreign and didn't understand English.

Halfway through the meal, a police car pulled up outside and two officers entered the café. Rosalyne watched, one hand on the knife inside her boot, always on guard.

"Hi Ken, any chance of coffees and something to eat? We've had to stay back. Something nasty's happened at Arnie's farm."

"Sure, Hector, pour yourselves coffee, and I'll do you bacon and eggs."

When Hector carried the coffees over to a table, Rosalyne was studying them carefully. *Protectors from Evil, this mortal knows them.*

Patrick, the other officer, helped himself to sugar and gave a running commentary on what they had heard over the radio.

"Arnie had come out to see what the commotion was with his dogs and found three armed youths attacking them. He went for the youths and they turned on him, but something behind him knocked him to the ground, and when he got up, the youths lay dead, their heads chopped off and blood everywhere; the dogs were nowhere to be seen, and Arnie's in a right state. Sarge said it was a drugs gang from the Boro."

Ken topped some toasted rolls with the bacon and eggs and brought them round.

"You're a lifesaver, Ken. Who's the girl?"

"I don't know, she might have been at the fayre, or could be one of them foreigners from the other end of the village."

"Can't remember seeing her there. Looking at that costume, she's probably with the re-enactment groups," Hector remarked.

"Aye, there was a lot about."

Hector's radio burst into life.

"Patrick, they want us to check a van on the road behind the farm. Thanks, Ken. A quid fifty each? Are you sure that's enough?"

"Yes, I have to look after you lot."

"Cheers. Come on, Patrick, get a move on."

Both ran out of the café.

Ken locked the door and turned back to the girl, she

had finished both meals, and had curled up on the seat with her cloak wrapped round her.

"Look lass, you can't sleep here."

She looked up at this mortal. She couldn't understand it; she needed to stay here in this refuge. It was safe and she could regain her strength.

Ken weighed her up, she was bedraggled, lonely, and worn-out.

"Why don't you go home?" he asked.

Her body needed rest; she looked round, not understanding.

Ken had a thought and walked back through the café into his house and upstairs. The rooms there still had the previous owner's furniture in them, one room had a bed. He turned the mattress on the bed and covered it with clean sheets, found pillows, a duvet and towels.

He hoped he was doing the right thing.

She was nearly asleep when he shook her lightly. Her eyes sprang open and knives appeared in her hands. Ken jumped back with fright. He had never seen anyone move as fast as she did, it was like a predator going for the kill.

Rosalyne, immediately recognising this mortal, sheathed the knives and relaxed. I must show this mortal I mean it no harm, she thought. She reached up and touched its hand, then lowered her arm, her eyes starting to close again.

Ken pulled her hand gently, then gestured her to follow him. She rose, collected her weapons, and followed him through the door. Upstairs, Ken turned on the light switches and showed her the toilet and bathroom on the landing. In the room, he pointed to her then the bed. She seemed to understand, then he left her and returned to the café, tidied up, and switched everything off.

Lying in bed, Ken wondered about the girl, had she been near Arnie's farm? He had seen enough weapons to know that hers were real, and, she was definitely not part of the re-enactment groups; they wouldn't have pulled knives on him. This girl had displayed the actions of a born killer when he woke her.

The sound of movement from upstairs subsided and silence fell on the house, Ken fell asleep.

Six am Ken woke, another day and food to prepare. After a wash and shave, he dressed, entered the café, switched equipment on, and made himself breakfast. He was open before seven. Customers had already started arriving for their breakfasts. Ken, now busy, would have to wait for a quiet period before attending to the girl.

Towards mid-morning, Rosalyne woke and lay there studying the room. It was dirty and full of objects, but this mortal had given her food and shelter. Rising, she found the place to wash and eventually discovered how to use it. After dressing herself, she would now find out more about this place of refuge before continuing her task. Leaving most of the weapons, she picked up the sword, descended the stairs and walked round the mortal's home inspecting everything. A lot cleaner, this must be living space for the mortal, she thought, then her senses detected the aroma of cooking and followed it.

Rosalyne entered the café.

Ken realised that something had happened when the hubbub of noise behind him suddenly stopped. Silence greeted him as he turned.

Standing in his doorway like a giant warrior, was the girl. She had the face of an Elf, the eyes, almond shaped, green and piercing. The gold crown upon her head touched the top of the doorframe, long tresses of reddish gold hair lay across her broad shoulders onto an emerald green robe. Belts of gold, black and red, crossed between her breasts and fastened to the belt round her waist, and there, resting in her hand, was the large sword. The girl looked round and found her Mortal, held its eyes for a moment, then continued looking round the room. No evil here, some bad, but not evil.

Ken moved quickly and taking her hand, guided her to a table. "Sit here and I'll cook you something in a minute, I've two more customers to serve first."

Rosalyne, watched her Mortal work.

Ken finished the serving and cooked a meal for the girl. Placing it in front of her, he sat opposite. This vision before him was a complete transformation from the bedraggled girl who arrived last night. He looked into her eyes, thinking, I'm sure I know this girl, her face seems familiar. Something about her was resurrecting memories from deep inside his brain, old memories passed on to him through his ancestors.

Hector walked in. "Afternoon, Ken, coffee please." Then he noticed the girl. "Good lord, is that, that girl?"

"Yes, she stayed here all night. She's beautiful, quite a makeover, don't you think?"

Hector stared. "She's like a warrior. I wouldn't want to cross swords with her."

"It could be a set-up, like that old TV series Candid Camera."

"I hope not. The Sarge would go apeshit if I ended up on TV."

"Heard any more about last night?"

"Another of the gang was in that van but without a head on his shoulders; it was in his lap. The whole cab was dripping blood. Patrick threw up all over the place; he's getting counselling for shock." Hector collected his coffee and moved to a table outside.

Ken looked at the girl. She has the weapons, could she have done it? he wondered. Her eyes locked onto his for a moment and he smiled.

Rosalyne was a warrior, warriors did not smile, but a faint glimmer of a smile appeared in her eyes. Looking again at her Mortal, she thought there was something in this mortal that was different to the others; it recognised and accepted it, maybe that was why it smiled.

She stayed, watching the mortals that used this place, and most of all, her Mortal. Rosalyne could not understand this. Low ones that were slaves, served their masters and did not join in, it was forbidden. Yet, this one seemed to be a Master and Slave all at the same time.

What happened to the old world and its ways? She had to return to the Bridge and ask it questions.

The following morning, Rosalyne rose early, dressed, descended the stairs, and headed through the café towards the door.

Ken, already hard at work, crossed to her and bade her leave the weapons upstairs. On her return, he held her hands. "Take care," he said and kissed her fingers.

Rosalyne was startled by this kiss. At the door, she turned and looked again at her Mortal. Its actions are now aware of my rank and treats me as such, she thought. Did some of our people become mortal?

As she closed the door, vivid images of an ancient legend scrolled through Ken's memories, then he saw her…

Rosalyne arrived at the Bridge. "Bridge, let me pass."

"My Queen, your task is not yet complete."

"Bridge! I cannot find our people, all is strange out there."

"In what way, my Queen?"

"It is like before Evil destroyed everything, only Mortals and strange things are here."

"It cannot be, my Queen."

"It is. How long was I imprisoned?"

"Time spoke to me as you departed; it wished to know of you… The Warrior Queen, I replied… Time knew nothing of you, my Queen."

"Knew nothing of me! How long is it then, Bridge?"

"We do not know, my Queen."

Rosalyne sat down. "You mean, all our race are no more?"

"That may be so, my Queen."

"Bridge, I wish to return to my time."

"My Queen, that time no longer exists. We kept guard over your tomb until your people came to release you. Your people never arrived. Lightning released you…"

Rosalyne, the Queen of Warriors, sat in silence. "What of my Mortal, is it one of our people?"

"My Queen, we cannot say of that mortal, it will be for you to decide."

"Then I have failed my people."

"No, my Queen. You may carry on your work in this world, but, you will have to follow their rules, the rule of mortals."

"So be it, it seems I have no choice but to accept my destiny."

"My Queen, you have a choice, go back and perish, or remain here and survive."

Rosalyne looked at the Bridge. Her decisions were fraught with anger, hatred and frustration, frustration for her people that had abandoned her in this strange world, anger and hatred of the Evil that had caused it. With a heavy heart she spoke. "Bridge, I will remain here with this mortal. I wish you farewell."

"I also wish you farewell, my Queen."

Down through the clouds, rays of sunlight descended, lighting up the Queen and all her land, the Land of the Shires across the Bridge. She sat there looking, vowing that one day, she and her people would return and cross this Bridge to their rightful land. Evil would not then dare to enter the Queen's land. As evening approached, she slowly stood up and made her way back to the village.

Ken, on hearing the door open and seeing the girl looking wretched, came over, bowed, took hold of her hands and kissed them.

"My Rosalyne. My Queen of Warriors," he said in an Ancient tongue, and taking her hand, guided his Queen to her table.

Rosalyne, the Queen of all Elven Warriors halted and looked at her Mortal. This mortal called me by name, she thought, my name, Rosalyne, and in our tongue; only my people would know of this name and tongue. A smile crept over her face, illuminating her features. I am not alone, he is of my people.

STUNG
PAUL R JASPER

"You don't look very well."

"Thanks." I felt even worse now.

"Are you ill," the lady asked again, staring irritatingly into my eyes.

"Very!" I replied, causing her to step back, almost falling off the curb and under the oncoming bus.

"You should see a doctor," she advised, moving nimbly away and waving for rescue.

The double decker swung past her high heels and sucked her through the opening doors as if a street sweeper was removing rubbish off the street. But she was no white trash, far from it. Her clothes and make-up were immaculate, painstakingly applied to conceal her age.

A line of grumbling pensioners followed her shimmering pink coat, complaining she had pushed in, but unable to speak up or move fast enough to stop her.

My bus wasn't for another ten minutes, but I suddenly had the urge to follow her. I had stood here for the past six months without a pleasant word from anyone, let alone a voice of concern.

I flashed my bus pass and stepped on board just as the doors were closing.

"Have you lost your mind?" the driver ranted, like I was one of the annoying school kids he had just off loaded.

I muttered an apology, but I must be crazy catching a bus to the wrong side of the valley. I was slightly scared, but at the same time invigorated by the feelings of a tantalising chase.

I looked around at the glum faces packing the lower seats and realised I would have to climb the spiralling steps for the first time in years. My nostrils were sniffing like a foxhound following a trail, but I wasn't brave enough to bloody my nose. I quickly shuffled onto the nearest seat and stared intensely at my woman looking out the front window.

In the bright light no makeup could hide her age. She was much older than my young wife, but she seemed to care about my wellbeing, something that was brushed aside at home with the annoying mantra, "It's alright for you – I still have to work."

I carefully rolled a coin along the floor and shuffled forward to pick it up.

She turned slightly to see what had made the seats rattle.

"Don't come any closer," she warned in a dominatrix voice.

"I've just dropped some money," I mumbled nervously.

"Stay away – I don't want your germs."

"No – I don't have any. The doctor says I'm suffering from Post Work Depression," I quickly explained, causing my latest infatuation to burst out laughing and release the tight grip of her handbag.

"Are you sure that's what he said? Is that like Post Natal Depression without the nappies and crying baby to worry about?" She grinned at a young lady bouncing a child on her knee. The teenage mum was the only other person upstairs and too preoccupied to listen.

"It's serious," I moaned. "The doctor's given me pills."

"I'm sorry," smiled the lady, beckoning me to sit closer as she shuffled along the seat. Her red, shiny shoes remained pointed forward and her pleated skirt perfectly aligned. "Have you always followed women?" she asked, almost flirting with her eyes.

"No. No, I don't. I was a teacher. I had every hour planned in fine detail, but now I don't know what to do with myself."

"You're a wasp when you should be a bee."

"Pardon?" I said, wondering if I had missed the beginning of a joke.

"Wasp – Bee," she repeated with an exaggerated frown turning to a clown-like smile.

"You mean I worry too much?"

The woman half nodded and stared out into the street below.

"My name's Peter," I smiled, holding out my hand.

The women reluctantly opened her handbag and pulled out a pair of gleaming white gloves. My arm wavered in the air while she slipped them on and finally shook my hand with the words, "Rosie."

"I'm depressed, not contagious," I joked, but it wasn't very funny and I wasn't really laughing. Ever since I left work nobody had been anywhere near me. My old friends were just my work colleagues and they were too busy to find time for me. I was out the loop, and already out of date.

"Do you always shake people's hands with gloves?" I asked as she put them neatly back in her bag.

"Only strangers, but the Queen Mother used to go to bed in hers," Rosie insisted.

I laughed, but she seemed to be serious.

"I'm leaving now," she announced, standing up to ring the bell with the end of a pencil.

"Is this where you work?" I asked as she squeezed past with only the scent of her perfume touching my body.

"I'm meeting Laura, my daughter," she explained. "She won Miss Teesside at just nineteen."

"I would love to meet her," I grinned.

"That's what they all say." Rosie frowned like I was the worst kind of wasp, ready to sting her daughter like other men had done.

"I'm only being friendly," I called as Rosie descended the stairs before the bus had even stopped.

The girl with the baby quickly followed, not wanting to be left alone with me. I couldn't blame her. I didn't want to be with me.

The bus shuddered to a halt and I watched Rosie step off and head towards the shops. She glanced up and slid her finger across her lips.

What did it mean? Was she telling me to keep quiet or blowing a kiss? She was like the Pied Piper, leading me on a journey I couldn't resist.

The bus began to shake as it slowly moved back into the stop-start traffic. I quickly pressed the bell. I needed to see her again.

The bus driver was in no hurry to stop so soon, particularly for me, and continued driving until he reached 'Second Hand Row', a chain of charity shops littering the outskirts of the city. I had never stepped inside one until three months ago when sheltering from the rain, but now they were part of my daily routine, something to bide the winter days and even to find a bargain. I had bought my wife a mixing bowl for a pound last week but I couldn't imagine Rosie visiting a charity shop. She would be expensive to take out. I fumbled through my coat pocket to see how much money I had, but I couldn't feel my wallet. I still had my keys and phone but my bus pass and every penny I had was gone!

Suddenly the Pied Piper's face flashed before me. Rosie had picked my pocket!

She couldn't be far from here. She was meeting her beautiful daughter and probably hiding out in one of the bars or cafés invading the high street.

I couldn't run any more, but I was moving with fire in my stomach. I was furious. She had hypnotised me with her white gloves, like an illusionist distracting my attention while leaving no fingerprints.

I staggered into a Wetherspoon's, holding my side and gasping the pungent air. The alcoholics had arrived early, hiding cheap stout behind a hearty breakfast. My thief was not going to be here!

I stepped back onto the pavement, near Rosie's final stop. There was a bakery and coffee shop opposite. I crossed over and glanced into Greggs without losing a stride, then sneaked into Costa. It was larger than my usual, but had the same segregation. Single people escaping the four walls of their home to fill an empty table made for four. I never noticed them when I chatted to my wife, but drink alone and you realise you're not alone, but still as lonely.

I glanced around then retreated. There was another Coffee House further up the high street. I would try that, but I wasn't holding out much hope. It was starting to spot with rain and I had no way of getting home. I quickly sheltered in a shop foyer and dialled my wife. She wasn't doing to like this one bit. I held the phone at arms length…

"…yes, Julie, I know… It was stolen… I don't know how… no money… I need you to pick me up… I'm sorry, Julie… Skipper Lane… Yes, that Skipper Lane… Okay… I'm sorry, love."

I put the phone back in my pocket and took a deep breath. I had fifteen minutes to think of a reason why I would be in the middle of Middlesbrough in the pouring rain – rain which was now bouncing off the road like hailstones on a trampoline, but through the torrent I suddenly saw the pink glow of Rosie's coat on the back of a chair. She wasn't hiding away, but sat alone in the window of a French restaurant.

I quickly zoomed in with my phone to take a fuzzy still of her thieving face before rushing across to confront her.

Rosie stared up from her empty cup and didn't seem surprised to see me enter the café looking like a drowned rat.

"Are you still following me," she asked, clinging to her handbag once more.

"I thought you were seeing your daughter?" I answered with a question, trying to prove she was not someone to trust.

"I am. Laura's at the counter paying the bill."

I turned and noticed an overweight women with a button nose trapped between two chubby cheeks. She was no beauty queen and Rosie was obviously a liar.

I rubbed my feet on the mat and tried to stay calm. "I've lost my wallet and wondered if you had picked it up by mistake?" I asked quietly.

"No," she smirked, sliding her handbag under the table and into the safety of her lap.

"Perhaps it fell into your bag," I suggested, parking an extra chair at the table.

"Get away," Rosie cried. "My daughter's a traffic warden and she'll sort you out."

Now that I could believe, but I wasn't moving without a fight.

"I want to see what you're hiding," I mouthed, putting my hand under the table.

"Laura, help!" Rosie screamed, causing the whole restaurant to stop and stare.

The wooden floorboards shook as Laura's oversize thighs pounded between the tables, her black hair scraped back like a sumo wrestler and her baggy tee shirt rippling between the diners' heads like the moving of a waterbed.

"I just want to check inside your handbag," I pleaded, taking hold of the handle just as the gigantic Laura placed her fat fingers on the rim of my chair and tilted it back.

"Get your hands off my mother," she whispered, staring down at me like a nightclub bouncer who didn't need to raise her voice.

"Not before I get my wallet," I squealed, pulling at the handbag with all my strength.

"I don't have it," Rosie yelled as the zip split and I toppled backwards, landing with my feet swaying in the air. The handbag emptied all over my face; lipsticks, powders and even pill pots landed like blows to my head, until a soft pair of white gloves glided past and landed on the dirty floor.

Laura lifted the chair back up and hauled me to my feet.

"You'll pay for a new bag, or I'm calling the police."

"Call the police," I dared, sitting back down with my arms folded.

"If you were a younger man I would crush you," she revealed before dragging me outside and dumping me on a soaking bench.

Everybody was staring, but I didn't care. Laura was a 21st century Fagin, using old ladies to rob and steal. I needed backup because the mean queen must have my wallet.

I moved further down the street and waited for them to leave.

"Peter. Peter. Get in before you die of pneumonia," shouted my wife from the opening window of her car. "What are you playing at? You're soaking wet!" she wailed, like I was a small child.

"I was following someone. I was hoping you could help," I explained.

"Shut the door. I'm meant to be in a meeting, not driving the streets looking for you. Some of us still have work!"

That was always her punchline, transforming my fragile ego from father figure to hopeless layabout in the blink of an eye.

"Well? What's going on? Who are you following?"

This was finally my moment to explain everything – almost – admitting I had chased another women would have been matrimonial suicide…

"You confronted a little old lady in a café and ripped open her handbag!" Julie parroted in disbelief.

I lowered my head once more, almost touching my chest.

"I know you're depressed, but this is unbelievable. The bus driver was right – you are losing your mind."

"I know it sounds crazy, but she took it. I have her picture on my phone," I insisted, rifling through my pockets.

"Don't tell me she's taken your mobile as well," my wife scorned, shaking her head like a dog after a bath.

"No. It must have fallen out when I was tipped over," I decided, still frantically searching my pockets.

"Unbelievable. That phone will cost hundreds to replace and your pension won't cover it," Julie moaned, turning the car around so sharply I was flung against the passenger window. "Go back in the café and see if it has been handed in," she ordered, slamming on the brakes and shoving me out the door.

Luckily two new diners had replaced Rosie in the restaurant window. They were smiling and the manager wanted to keep it that way. He raced to the door and blocked my entrance.

"What do you want?" he asked, straightening his tie and puffing out his chest.

"I've lost my phone. I wondered if any one had handed it in?"

"Your phone?" he questioned. "I thought it was your wallet you lost."

"It was, but I must have lost my phone in here. If I could just ask those ladies."

"No. Not after last time. We haven't had any phone handed in," the manager calmly insisted as he walked me a few feet back to my car. "Go to the police station and report them missing, before I report you," he added as I meekly agreed.

"No. He can ring from home," my wife interrupted, as she drove off before I could fasten my seatbelt. If I didn't know her better I would think she was trying to kill me!

"Wait. That's them," I yelled, blocking Julie's vision with my pointing finger.

"Put your arm down," she roared as Rosie caught my wife's eye and smiled like a clown in a horror movie.

To my surprise Julie stopped the car and stepped out as if she too had been bewitched.

I peered between the headrests as Laura the colossus opened her arms and lifted Julie into the air! My wife looked back at the car as I sank into the seat. I told her they were violent. There was nothing I could do. I tilted the rear mirror slightly to sneak a peek. Julie was back on the ground and squeezing under their umbrella in deep conversation.

I could rely on Julie to sort it out. She organised everything at home and was no fool in the office. My wife would quickly realise what had happened.

"I've sorted it," Julie announced, eventually returning to the driver's seat.

"You've got my wallet!" I said excitedly.

"No stupid! I've apologised. I've stopped them from filing charges by telling Laura you're mentally ill," Julie tutted, looking at me with disgust. "As a favour Rosie has offered to find your wallet and phone."

"Oh, she's Miss Marple now!" I said sarcastically.

"And who are you? Peter the Stalker? Because I was so embarrassed. I went to school with Laura. She used to be a beauty queen…"

I half listened to my wife's childhood memories of Rosie and her glorious cooking and waited for the enviable one-liners.

"They thought you were my father. I told them I do all the work…"

But as I closed my eyes to snooze I was blindsided by the words, "I've had enough of you chasing other women. I want a divorce…"

After a restless night I returned to the bus stop with ten pounds sewn into my coat pocket and a list of bedsits to check out on the other side of town.

Strangely, I didn't feel any different to yesterday, but that might be the effect of the pills. Nothing seemed to matter anymore.

I noticed the usual faces waiting under the bus shelter except for a scruffy man stepping out of line.

"Are you the stalker," he asked, as if my mug shot had been plastered on every poster and Facebook page.

"What?"

"Did you follow Rosie?"

"Do you know her?"

"Everyone knows Rosie, but she's not well today. She's recovering from an attack by a giant wasp!"

I sighed and joined the end of the queue, but the homeless man continued to follow.

"I recognised you from your bus pass," he announced, pulling it out of a plastic bag.

"Where was it?" I asked, snatching it out of his dirty hand.

"Who knows? Best not to ask too many questions," he stuttered, before producing my wallet, as if pulling a white rabbit from a magician's hat!

I quickly peered inside. Nothing had been taken.

"Did I drop it getting on the bus," I asked as guilt swarmed around my ashen-face.

"It was found. What more can I say," he whispered knowingly as he once again put his hand in a smelly bag and pulled out a black phone.

I stood silently for a second until my shaking finger unlocked the handset, revealing a glowing picture of my soon to be ex.

"Did Rosie give you these," I asked angrily.

"Maybe," he began to weep, "but take my advice – be careful who you stalk next time, because sooner or later you'll get stung!"

WHAT REMAINS OF ROGER
TRICIA LOWTHER

No one expects an old woman to climb a safety fence. Especially at the top of a waterfall. But at seven o'clock on this wet Wednesday morning there's no one about to stop her.

Annie doesn't think of herself as old.

"Seventy is the new forty," she'd told their Nicola last week when she'd asked what Annie wanted to do for her birthday. It's the kind of thing the family would expect her to say. You're supposed to hide pain. She wonders what they'll think when they hear what she's done.

High Force is in full flow, a deafening, spectacular display of raw power and beauty. The Tees thunders down the ravine, blasts into the dark, whirling basin, as it has done since long before she was born and will continue to do, long after her death.

She knew the top of the falls was fenced off these days,

to stop people from walking out onto the rocks, but she hadn't expected the bottom gate to be locked too.

It's easy to climb. There are holes in the mesh where others have pushed their feet through to stand on the wooden rails. Annie has shrunk a little in the last few years but she's tall enough to pull herself up and get one leg over without too much trouble. She carefully pulls the other leg up behind it and drops down onto the steps. She tugs the zip of her waterproof up under her chin, pushes grey springy curls back under her hood, and pulls the drawstring tighter. The final stretch before she says her last goodbye.

She thinks about the first time she came here, in 1969, nervous about spending the weekend with Roger. He'd borrowed a small tent from a friend.

They'd been seeing one another for three months or so. Annie was studying at Durham University, out dancing every weekend in her white boots and mini skirt with Margot, Rosemary and the others. They'd all been high on independence, evenings spent crammed onto one of their beds gossiping, laughing, drinking cocoa late at night. The pill had just become available and fab bands like The Who, Pink Floyd and Free played at the students' union, Dunelm House – a controversial new Brutalist building. It was where she met Roger.

He'd travelled from his home town of Stockton with two friends who wanted to see Procul Harum.

"Your one's gorgeous," Margot had whispered to her at the end of the night, and he was – tall and slim with dark collar length hair, but it was his quirky humour and air of quiet humility that had endeared him to her. She always loved to dance, but Roger introduced her to a love of long, lazy rambles through the countryside.

They'd picked a hidden spot on the other side of the waterfall to camp, a high, rocky outcrop flanked by bushes. It was long before the fences, the safety signs and admission charges. She'd thought it might be cold, uncomfortable, awkward, and it had been all of those things. It had also been perfect. The door of the tent faced out across the river. They'd sat outside on the flat rock, legs dangling over the edge, and eaten hard boiled eggs, lumps of cheese, apples and fruit loaf, then drank cheap wine before zipping up for the night, hands cold at first under each other's clothes. The roar of the water lessened their inhibitions like music, a romantic backdrop as they loved one another, shyly at first, then with an intensity that still made her abdomen tug and twitch when she thought of it all these years later. She'd felt deliriously alive. She couldn't think of a better place to end things.

At the top of the steps she pauses. The jagged, moss covered rocks don't scare her, but she's breathless after the climb. Perhaps she should have brought a walking stick, be daft to slip at the last minute and end up with a broken ankle, or worse. She scrambles over the fence and treads carefully across wet stones toward the higher centre ground. In front of her the rock drops away, gouged out by the relentless river. She looks over to the bushes where they'd camped all those years ago, sees her younger self looking back, full of the early morning that belonged to her then, her view, her waterfall. So much life ahead.

Later there'd be visitors. Kids would clamber over the boulders below, anxious parents yelling at them to be careful. Unaware of her tragedy, her loss, her grief.

As close to the torrent as she can get, she leans into a rock, hugs the small bulge under her coat. Her words disappear into the noise. "Here we are again, Roger, just like the first time."

She removes the urn from her inside pocket. How can there be so little of him? She'd chosen an environmentally friendly model that would break down naturally in water, like he'd have wanted. She sniffs, wipes her soft, lined cheeks, then smiles at the memory of Roger's laugh when their little granddaughter had called her wrinkles 'stripes'.

She holds him to her heart. "Where did the time go?"

She lifts the lid, pinches a tiny bit of the grainy substance inside and touches it to her lips.

"We had a good life together, didn't we, Roger? Unremarkable, but good." She nods to herself. "We had golden years."

She doesn't kid herself, it wasn't all good, but they'd done alright, raised a family, bought their own home, travelled abroad on holidays. They'd been privileged. Seems like they'd had it better than their children's generation, what with pollution, climate change and the nuclear threat raising its ugly head again. She thought they'd gone past all that, but she'd learned that change was not a progression. Battles were never won. They had to be refought. Like Roger, with the cancer. He'd beaten it twice and still it came back, got him in the end.

"You wouldn't want to be scattered or gently sprinkled, would you, Roger? Given the chance you'd jump off the edge, dive right into it." The others had said their goodbyes at the church. She'd been numb.

"You know, I still don't believe you've gone. Not really."

She bounces on the spot, swings her arm a couple of times. Then she hurls what remains of Roger into the sky.

The urn somersaults mid-air, and his ashes fly from it, seeming momentarily to form into a shape, a heart, she fancies, before dropping to become one with the water.

For a fragment of a moment she wants to plunge after him, into that surge of terror and exhilaration. She imagines how it would feel to shatter, like the river, into a million drops, to scream her rage and relief, and be re-formed, with every particle shaken, charged and transformed. She watches the water rush away from her, like years.

THE TRIUMPH HERALD
GEOFFREY MARSH

Perkins felt a frisson of excitement run through his body as he winged his way over Victoria Bridge across the Tees in the recently released, brand new Triumph Herald. He always felt better escaping from the grimy south bank of the river to the pleasanter environment of Stockton and especially Norton. He was driving it from the distributors in Middlesbrough to his small Triumph dealership in Norton. The traffic was light and the car sped along Stockton's broad High Street. To him it drove like a dream. He manoeuvred it gently into the centre of his modest forecourt near the south end of Norton High Street. He gazed at it – it was a thing of beauty. The distributors had told him to try and sell it to a well-known person in the area – someone who drove a great deal on both sides of the river; they hoped it would encourage further orders. He had already contacted such a person, not that he would mention this inadvertent commercialism to her and he awaited her arrival eagerly and with some trepidation. She was the sort of customer he both valued and feared.

•

Maude, tallish, medium build, middle-aged, matronly, strode along the pavement of the gracious tree-lined Norton High Street. As a prominent and, she felt, valued member of this suburban village society she surveyed her world as an empress would her domain. Some of the locals acknowledged her with obvious respect and reverence. She nodded imperiously in their direction and strode regally on. Being from a successful and well-established Home Counties family, and a handsome young woman, she had been presented at Court in those halcyon days when such events pertained. She had met Digby at one of the balls afterwards. Those social events were so good for introducing nice gels like herself to young men with good prospects. Although Digby was from the north, his family had a successful shipping business on the River Tees and overall she was considered to have made a good match.

Digby's firm really flourished during the war as a result of an extremely lucrative contract to build 'landing ship tanks' for conveying the soldiers onto the Normandy beaches on D-Day. They made enormous profits. But after the war there was that unfortunate business when one of their merchant ships had gone down and a handful of lives were lost. The trades union people made an awful fuss and tried to sue the firm for negligent maintenance of the vessel and also made out it was overloaded. Digby employed quality legal people from London – friends from his Guardsman days – and it all blew over eventually, although the poor man did have one or two sleepless nights. Sadly, it did get into the newspapers and probably put paid to Digby's later potential knighthood. He finished up with an OBE but felt quite insulted and almost turned it down.

•

For her walk down the High Street Maude donned her pale green suit from Jaeger, skirt respectably below the knee, well concealing her protective directoires, important when getting in and out of motor vehicles. She rarely walked, except on country holidays, but she was going to collect her new car, an aptly named Triumph Herald.

She rather liked the High Street with its Georgian ambiance and mix of large and small houses. The narcissi were currently in bloom; Digby's father had donated them to the village many years ago. She personally knew most of the residents in the larger houses and those in the smaller ones knew her by repute. Lilian, her cook-housekeeper, lived in one of the smaller ones but she was unsure which. The boys always took the Christmas pudding that she herself had made and they said her house was very cosy inside and everyone seemed so cheerful and they laughed a lot.

All things considered, on this fine spring morning, Maude was content. She would never say that all was well in the world but she was quite happy, comfortable and satisfied with how things were for her.

•

Kevin Smithson – Smiggy to his mates – was flat out at 10am in his squalid bedroom in the rundown terrace house in the back streets of Norton. He awoke to the sound of his mum screaming from the bottom of the uncarpeted stairs imploring him to get up. He was in his usual foul mood. His head was throbbing and his mouth tasted of the residue of fags, alcohol, cannabis and sex – not the best state to be in prior to his important afternoon appointment. His mum would need their old Toyota to get to work at a distant Asda checkout, so he would have to go to it by bus. After a Marathon bar, some toast and a cuppa, Smiggy was soon slouching up Norton High Street. He was vaguely aware of an unusual pale blue car speeding towards the Green.

•

Perkins smilingly oiled his way across the forecourt towards Maude.

"Beautiful!" he exclaimed. For a fleeting moment Maude thought the weaselly fellow was being extremely personal, but his eyes had wandered towards the powder blue vehicle stationed solitarily on the forecourt.

"There she is!" he crowed; and for no reason she could think of a shiver of foreboding passed through her as she followed his adoring look at the car.

"A work of art!" he declaimed.

She ignored the eulogy.

"So this is it?" she said frostily. "Seems a bit small!"

"Ah! – Giovanni Michelotti, Italian stylist, demonstrating economy of scale."

Maude was inherently suspicious of Italians.

"You see before you, ma'am, a breakthrough in automotive innovation: the rediscovery of the chassis."

Maude was not impressed by this, to her, meaningless information.

He flung open the fairly wide driver's door.

"Easy access," he said.

She trusted this was not a reflection on her personal agility.

"It has wonderful brakes," he opined, "with an excellent stopping capability."

There was silence – Maude was used to cars being able to stop – what a silly man!

Perkins raised the bonnet reverentially to display to her the inventiveness of the very latest engineering science.

"Why are you doing that?" Maude said. "I never lift the bonnet."

She plumped down onto the driving seat, her chassis

and that of the car tolerating each other for the very first time.

"Comfortable, isn't it, grips you, holds you in."

Maude thought this was in rather poor taste, but let it pass.

"It has an amazingly tight turning circle."

She interpreted that as being able to execute u-turns in fairly narrow streets, obviating the need for that tedious three-point business.

Perkins thrust his head through the driver's window in unpleasant proximity to hers.

"You will find it has plenty of power – more than your old Rover, even with the smaller engine."

Maude failed to understand that but presumed he knew what he was talking about – and was glad to get rid of him.

She drove off and was soon travelling swiftly in top gear up the High Street. Perkins was right – it certainly went well. Suddenly she was horrified to see a little old lady tottering into the road across her path. Maude jammed on the splendid brakes and the low gravity of a chassis-ed car enabled the new tyres to grip the tarmac rigidly and skid to a halt. She felt the bumper hit the old lady and saw her tossed forward to fall motionless just clear of the by now thankfully stationary car. Glad of the wide door, Maude leapt out, hitched up her skirt, relieved that her directoires prevented exposing her thighs to the slowly assembling crowd around her, and examined her victim.

Dead to the world, no carotid pulsation, not breathing.

Maude rolled her over flat on her back, tore open her clothing, and kneeled down beside her. She counted down five ribs from the clavicle, placed the heel of her left hand to the left of the sternum, and – pressing very firmly at sixty pressures per minute with her right hand on top of her left – began the external cardiac massage she had once been taught at a WI evening. There was no immediate response. Noticing a surprisingly smartly dressed but languid-looking teenager in the small group that had gathered around, she ordered him to kneel down beside the woman's head, wipe the mucus from her mouth and start insufflation.

Fortuitously, Smiggy had picked up a rather sleazy girl at the Fiesta club the previous night so had been recently practised in mouth-to-mouth contact and even some insufflation; these thoughts flitted through his brain as he began his task.

"Nip her nose, boy!" Maude commanded. "To get the air to the lungs – one breath every ten seconds."

Obeying her orders, the youth began to introduce the resuscitative life-saving air into the old lady's chest. Slowly, slowly, pulses returned and spontaneous breathing commenced and became established. Maude felt quite proud of herself recalling being complimented on her technique by the instructors at the WI evening. The police and an ambulance arrived on the scene and the old lady was transported to the North Tees Hospital A&E department.

"We'll need a statement," the police officer demanded.

"Those skid marks suggest you were going rather fast."

"Oh dear," she said. "Well, I've no time now – I've got to be in court in fifteen minutes. Could you possibly come to The Towers at the top of Osbaldeston Drive at 8.45 this evening? It's the big house at the end. We will have dined by then."

The constable made a note of it and acquiesced reluctantly, saying it was a bit irregular; but she was who she was and he had actually done some court work with her.

"I know the house, ma'am – I once went to a charity evening there for the Lifeboats."

"I'll leave the gates open and make sure the dogs have been called in." Using the tight turning circle, Maude pirouetted in the road and proceeded to the Middlesbrough Magistrates Court.

The constable began taking a few witness statements, including one from Smiggy.

•

Assembled in the courtroom were the chairman of the Bench, two magistrates of whom Maude was one, plus the usual officers and policemen. Magistrates were chosen from amongst the respectable people on Teesside – worthy public-spirited folk like herself – people prepared to give their time freely for the common weal; certainly this was Maude's view.

The accused were mostly young, of limited education,

unemployed (unemployable, Maude would say) and often from fractured domestic settings. Feckless, careless people, she thought. Many of the charges related to minor theft, breaking and entering, speeding, drunk driving, drug offences, shop-lifting – those sort of things. Anything really serious was referred on to a higher court. Once in a while a respectable middle-class member of Teesside society would appear. The court would often be able to find exonerating circumstances and sentences would be minimal, or the case even dismissed. After all, these people weren't a drain on society – they actually contributed.

The afternoon session was composed of the usual detritus of ignorant young people from the poorer parts of Teesside, particularly from the south side of the river. How fortunate Maude felt to be resident a little to the north – Norton on the whole was quite a salubrious suburb. After her exertions en route she began to feel slightly somnolent when – to her astonishment – the callow youth from the accident appeared before them! This explained his wearing of a smartish suit in the middle of a working day. No tie though – typical of the slovenly youth these days. She sat stolidly on with her two colleagues.

Kevin Smithson was charged with careless driving; he had gone up a one-way street in the wrong direction late at night with no lights and smelling of alcohol. Smiggy looked at Maude hopefully – and gave her a conspiratorial wink. She ignored this impertinence, but did reflect on whether their joint resuscitation of the apparently dead woman implied a conflict of interest, and should she decline to adjudicate in his case? She decided she could continue.

The facts were read out. The constable concerned had all dates, times and his interview well recorded. Cut and dried: guilty. No leniency was shown by the Bench, especially by Maude, and he was quite heavily fined and his driving licence withdrawn for one year. On hearing the verdict, Smiggy glared at Maude. Retribution could be his!

Several more cases dwindled towards evening.

•

After court, Maude drove the car home steadily. She went up the long drive and entered the house.

Digby was petulantly awaiting her return. He looked over the top of his Times; he was glancing through the deaths.

"You're late," he said. "I told Lilian to hold dinner."

They processed into the dining room and took their places at each end of the long table. Lilian served the meal and poured some wine. Maude covered her glass.

"Only water, please, Lilian."

Digby raised an eyebrow.

"How's the new car?" he said.

"Fine," Maude said. "Seems to do what it says on the tin – goes very well."

A pause.

"Great cricket news – Edrich 98 not out at Lord's – teach those West Indians a thing or two."

Another pause.

"Nasty accident on the A1 north of Newcastle yesterday. Two dead on the road – people drive too fast. Should all be locked up and lose their licences forever."

"Yes," Maude said weakly.

Digby looked up at her in surprise; she usually acquiesced wholeheartedly with such strong opinions.

They had just finished and Lilian had served coffee when Maude heard the front door knocker.

"I'll go," she shouted to Lilian.

Maude walked along the Axminster-carpeted passage, head held high, and opened the heavy mahogany front door. There were two uniformed policemen on the step. Wearing their black helmets they reminded her of hooded crows.

"Come in," she said, and ushered them in to her book-lined study. She was rather proud of her literature collection, not that she had read much of it – for her, life was more about doing than just sitting reading; but the volumes looked very well and she had had them beautifully bound.

"I'm afraid I've bad news for you," the inspector began. "You'd better sit down."

She perched on the edge of her fine Sheraton armchair. The policemen squatted on two Hepplewhite chairs.

"The woman you hit seemed a little shocked but in quite

reasonable condition when she arrived at the hospital. However, they decided to admit her for overnight observation and some X-rays. She died suddenly in the radiology department."

"Oh how dreadful," Maude heard herself saying. She shrank back into her chair.

"The X-rays showed two fractured ribs just to the left of the sternum, so the radiology staff were reluctant to give her external cardiac massage. The emergency surgical team was summoned but by the time they arrived there was nothing they could do; she had died."

There was an unearthly silence except for the ticking of the fine antique longcase clock in the hall. Each person reflected in a different way on this information.

"What now?" said Maude solemnly.

"I'm afraid this has extremely serious implications for your driving."

Another silence – more meditation.

"Your skid marks suggest you were travelling at about 45 miles per hour just prior to hitting the old lady. There were two or three witnesses who maintain you were speeding up the High Street. The young man who helped you will be called as a witness; he thought you could be doing 50 miles per hour."

The inspector stood up.

"Maude Matthews, I am ordering you to attend Stockton central police station at 10am tomorrow where you will be formally charged with an offence under the road traffic act. You will be given a date to attend

Middlesbrough Magistrates Court. You may bring a legal representative with you if you wish. In view of the fatality, your case will almost certainly be referred to a higher court by the magistrates. A vehicle transporter will pick up your car tomorrow morning and will convey it to expert mechanics who will examine it for any defects in the controls."

The policemen left.

Maude climbed her beautiful staircase and went to bed, but not to sleep. In the morning she wrote a letter of resignation from the Bench. The serene and ordered world of twenty four hours ago was collapsing around her.

No fault was found in the Triumph Herald.

•

As Maude was being driven across the Tees to the court, she wondered how long it would be before she was once again free to do that herself. Certainly it would not be in a Triumph Herald. Digby had already sold it.

On the same day Smiggy was crossing the Tees by bus. He too was going to attend court.

His grin was as wide as the river.

GIRL IN THE WATER
PETER MARTIN

My hotel room looked as bad as I felt, a drab mess. I'd gone to lie down but missed and hit the floor hard. Riz, however, wasn't impressed as he crawled out from my jacket pocket.

"Hey Riz, I'm gunna lie down... 'ere ya go, Riz, I'll let ya out of my pocket..."

He was clearly irritated, but then I couldn't blame him, I had almost squashed him.

"No, I'm just gunna fall and crush ya instead." His sarcasm continued as he scurried up the leg of the bed, so he could peer down at me.

"What happened out there, Bren? Ya got yer ass handed to ya."

"I don't know." I had no idea why I couldn't handle a water ghoul. Though, it felt like this wasn't an ordinary pest control.

"Ya don't know? Gee, how fantastic. Remember: no extermination, no money!" Riz started yelling again, though to any listener, it would've sounded like a rat squeaking.

I tried to drown him out by focusing on my own thoughts. To sort this, I was going to have to go through everything that had happened…

Yesterday.

My phone rang, breaking my blissful dreamless sleep. I reached for it, but being groggy, grabbed the remains of last night's meal. When I finally caught it, I'd hardly spoken when the caller shoved their voice down my ear. However rude it seemed, they were dangling a job offer in front of me. You only had to look and smell the inside of my car, my temporary home, to know that I'd be accepting this job whatever it was. Minutes later I was heading north. My destination? Teesside.

My employer had ordered me to meet him at his workplace: Preston Farm industrial estate. We were travelling up the A19, barely twenty minutes out when Riz woke up in his little nest in my glove compartment. I don't wake up all that well but my assistant – his title when we're on good terms – makes the worst hangover look like a pleasant morning. Today was no different.

"Argh! Why is yer engine so loud?" he squeaked, crawling onto the dash and looking out. "What's the job?"

"Water ghoul," I replied, watching for directions.

"Water ghoul? That's better than that two-timing crap." Riz hated me working for paranoid couples accusing each other of this and that.

Before long I pulled into an ordinary car park of an ordinary factory. I hadn't even got out before a grinning bearded face was pressed against my window.

"You the guy I ordered?" he barked.

"Mr Grant?" As I diverted attention, Riz scurried back into my pocket.

"Please, call me Wes." Wes opened my door and stuck his hand in my face. My first instinct was to punch him but I held back. Begrudgingly I shook his hand only to be pulled into a hug. He patted my back before releasing his gorilla-like grip.

"Now we can put this nonsense to rest," he said, beaming.

"Nonsense?"

"Yes, nonsense. Come on and I'll explain." Wes beckoned me to follow him into his factory.

The explanation was brief. Due to a lot of his staff seeing something strange in the River Tees, his workforce had plummeted. He wanted his staff back so I was hired to fix things. From the description earlier I knew it was a water ghoul so I quickly excused myself, as he insisted on being very hands on in an unpleasantly literal way.

Once we were outside, Riz spoke up.

"Well, he was friendly…"

"Too friendly… I think he tried to break my ribs."

"You'll live, and with the right setup this should be easy

money for us." Riz rubbed his paws together, drooling in excitement.

"Let's get this job done first before you waste our cash." I put extra emphasis on 'our' – one day it might sink in. Now, knowing my target, time to prep my gear.

In my line of work, the best tools mean everything but for me, I'm forced to improvise wherever and whenever possible. Opening the boot of my car to look at my inventory, Riz quickly jumped in and started examining things. He may be a rat with an otherworldly entity inside him but he had an eye for quality. He tossed a few bits to the side before pulling out a small bag and rummaged through it.

"Perfect." He dragged a few coin-shaped charms out and then re-tied the pouch and gestured for me to take it as he went back to sorting. Trusting his knowledge, I attached the pouch to my tool belt. A few minutes later, Riz found a couple of healing charms. Lastly, he pushed a small sealed box towards me, smirking as he did. I couldn't hide my disgust when I peeked under the lid.

"I forgot about those…" Begrudgingly I pocketed the box, cursing it as I did. For the stakeout, I had chosen the point where the shore was closest to Wes's factory. With everything set, one night was all I needed. Now it was time to check into the cheapest room I could find.

"By the way, Riz," I said, turning to my little companion as he made his way out of the car. "You might want to block your nose later."

"Why? My sense of smell is one of my best features!"

"You'll see…"

A few hours later, we pulled up back to the factory. I double-checked my gear as I got out and Riz got comfortable in my pocket as always. The river was fairly quiet by the time me and Riz stood on the bank, with only the ambient noise of faraway cars and machines stopping it from being a chilling silence. Riz hadn't bothered taking my advice from earlier about his nose; I could hear him gagging. I couldn't imagine what he was smelling as the putrid stench of rotting plant life and festering waste was overpowering. I looked around for signs of life but no other humanoid shapes moved. From my tool belt I removed the ornate box and took out the contact lenses from within. Each lens was a nasty parasitic creature, allowing the wearer to see in the dark like all nocturnal hunters. I was hesitant though, already I could feel it moving in my hand. This was going to hurt.

"Just get them in yer head already!" Riz grunted as he made his way from my pocket to the ground. "Ya've gotta get this job done so stick 'em in and be done with it." He scurried over to a pile of rocks, using the added height to get a good grasp of the area.

"It's easy for you to say! You try sticking these in!" How I wished I could have afforded the high tech approach.

"I don't need to. I can see everything in the dark, unlike you but just carry on without them, see how you like fumbling around blind."

"Fine!" I lifted the first lens to my eye, and the lens's

little tentacle-like appendages stiffened, pointing to my moist eye. I gulped, and slammed it into my eye.

The pain transcended belief, imagine sticking a toilet brush into your eye socket and wiggling it around. The effects kicked in straight away as the night lit up. The Tees itself took on an ethereal beauty. After a moment I finally had the lenses in both bloody eyes. Riz took position as a sentry while I wiped my eyes. Now I had to act as bait.

We didn't have to wait long for the water ghoul to take the bait. The sound of rushing water tinged with the anguished cries of children, heralded her appearance. A shadow formed in the water, ominously bubbling as a large shape bulged up. Two yellow orbs glared outwards, rolling around the shape till they locked onto me. The shape then stretched out, revealing a humanoid figure, that of a little girl with green skin and long dark emerald hair that flowed into the waters below. The girl was wearing the muddy and tattered algae-stained remains of a dress.

I staggered backwards, through the dirt, putting distance between me and her. I stared at her, and she just stared back with those luminous yellow eyes. Something immediately felt off. In every other case, you could feel the malice as if there was someone breathing down your neck, but here I felt nothing.

"Bren! What are ya waiting for!" Riz snapped from his safe spot.

My hand idled near my tool belt but neither me or the water ghoul moved. Was she waiting for me to make the first move? A stone then hit me in the back of the head, and I knew that Riz, the git, had thrown it to get my attention.

"We've got a job to do, Bren! Just get rid of the brat."

I was going to throw an insult at Riz but the water ghoul surprised us both. It stretched its hand out towards me and made gurgling sounds. I would say it tried to talk but all that came out was a mixture of noises that sounded more at home on a backing track for an artsy horror movie. It started creeping closer to me, still muttering. I tried to listen to what it was saying. Maybe it didn't want to rip me apart, maybe it just needed a hug. I was wrong, it was gibberish.

"Sorry, I don't understand…"

As soon as I said those words, I was screwed. The water ghoul trembled violently and her face contorted into a mix of rage and despair. Before I could react, a jet of water blasted me to the muddy shore where my back rammed into the rocks. I tried to exhale the pain but my leg was grabbed by tendrils of flowing water and I was flung to the opposite shore, where sharp stones ripped into my face. With no time to recover, I was dragged backwards and pummelled by dozens of short water spouts shaped like fists. Amidst all of this I heard Riz's voice but couldn't make out what he was yelling. Another blast hit my face, forcing a rancid liquid into my mouth, giving me a taste of the dirty river. Once more I was tossed to the opposite shore but given a moment to catch my breath, the air tasting like a salivating buffet compared to the river water I coughed up. I turned around just as the water ghoul latched onto my limbs and pulled me up into the air. Her grip on me tightened as more jets of water struck me from underneath. Of course I tried to struggle, but there wasn't a lot I could do. Then I caught sight of something, something very surprising indeed. Out of the corner of my eye I spotted Riz holding up something that glittered in a way that objects should never do. Before I could react, an image broke into my mind, that of a little girl in a mirror, wearing a pretty white dress. The girl was miserable and behind her, hands rubbing her shoulders, was a grinning man with an eye for innocent things. I was forced back to reality by the sound of thunder and I splashed down into the river. The water ghoul, hurt but still alive, retreated into a now raging Tees. Being pulled downstream added to my already battered body, as I was dragged against the concrete banks underneath Victoria Bridge. A little luck graced me and I got snagged by rubbish near the barrage. Riz woke me up by raking his claws over my face.

"Get up, will ya!" His bedside manner was atrocious. Having jumped into the water after me, he was a literal drowned rat. By his side was my tool belt. He explained he'd retrieved it, after the water ghoul had ripped it off, and used it to attack in my stead. His aim sucked however so he'd just wounded it. Still, I was alive and reunited with my tool belt which meant I could begin the laborious process of healing myself.

Right, I was back to where I started, me on the floor, Riz up high.

"Ya finished down there?"

"Yeah, I'm done." Well, actually I wasn't. I still needed to piece this together. From the way she acted and the way she was trying to communicate, going as far to try and establish a telepathic connection, she was no water ghoul. She was a wraith, a trapped spirit that was twisted with anger and pain. Her subconscious had possessed a loathsome water ghoul to give her a body once more and along with it their water manipulating abilities. She had been desperate for help before she died and that was all her spirit wanted now... She just got upset when no one understood her.

"That bastard..." The person who was responsible for the death of this little girl, or at least, all of the abuse, was also staring me in the face. In fact he'd had his hands all over me.

"Who's a bastard?" Riz was still sat there, listening to all my murmurings, with an eyebrow raised. I explained everything as clearly as I could make it. Riz buried his head with his paws. I couldn't tell if he was crying because of the girl or because we weren't going to be paid.

"Why can't jobs with good money ever be simple?"

"Yeah, shame about the poor girl."

"Well, that goes without saying, the man is a walking cesspool who needs a good kickin' but still, that money." Nice to see Riz had his priorities right.

"Money is going to have to wait." My plan now was to sleep, let the healing charms finish and do a quick library check to confirm everything.

I went to the library in Thornaby town centre around three, got on the net and hit up the Evening Gazette's archives; it didn't take me long to find what I was looking for – unfortunately. The story confirmed my hunches. I recognised the girl from the photos instantly and then the pictures of her grinning stepdad, Wes. She was never found, so despite suspicions, Wes escaped punishment, till now anyway.

A few hours later and we were parked outside the factory, waiting for Wes to leave. He saw us first and headed right to us.

"Sorted?" He was too close again. The smell of expensive aftershave mixed with depraved sweat wafted into my nose. I felt bad for Riz, this was worse than the river.

"You bet. Want to see what it was?" Swallowing my bile, I threw my arm around him best I could and started leading him, well, dragging him to the river.

"Won't take long, will it? Got a hot date tonight, if you know what I mean."

I rolled my eyes as far back as they would allow.

"Won't take long at all…" I let go of him as we stood before the river. If Wes was any smarter, he might, and I'll stress that 'might', have sensed the dread that hung in the air like a noose on a gallows. He was standing tantalisingly close to the water's edge but kept on taking a step away from it as the water leapt at him.

Riz was also getting restless.

"Bren, get the money first. Bren get the money first," he kept repeating.

I relented and was about to bring it up when sod's law kicked in. The wraith's head had risen above the water and saw Wes. To say all hell broke loose would be fitting if, instead of fire, you pictured water. I was blasted backwards and lost sight of Wes in the foam. Everything became calm again.

"Is that it?" Riz slowly slid his head out of my pocket to see but hid again as Wes burst out of the water, bloodied and gasping for every breath.

"Help… Help…" He was holding onto the riverbank with every ounce of strength he had left. He was a pitiful sight. I'm not going to lie, I was looking forward to what I was about to do. I stood up and walked over to him. As I neared, I raised my right leg and swung it down with everything I could muster. My boot connected with his pudgy face with a satisfying crunch. The force of the kick jolted him away from the shore, into the waiting arms of his victim. She was stood there like an avenging angel, relishing the torture and returning all her pain and agony to where it came from. Before Wes could have screamed, she'd plunged them both into the water. Calm fell once more. Five minutes passed and nothing else happened.

"Now it's over."

Riz heard what I said and ventured out.

"A tough one to explain," he muttered.

"Not my job."

A light caught my eye: a little girl stood in the middle of the river, floating an inch above the water. She was instantly recognisable from the pictures in the paper. She smiled at me and mouthed the words 'thank you' then was gone.

In the days after, the local paper jumped on Wes's disappearance and subsequent appearance of blood in the water. Theories flew like a murder of crows, ranging from secret government agencies to aliens. Once the police found his stash of child porn and other sick junk, everyone became less interested in how he'd died, being glad he was dead. I, on the other hand, was sadly right back where I'd started.

"No money again…" Riz sighed as he lay in a depressed heap on my dash.

"There'll be a job for us somewhere around here… If there isn't, fancy seeing if there's hidden treasure in that buried street in Stockton?"

"Treasure, you say?" Riz's ears picked up. He looked mischievous again. "Step on it, Bren!"

MINDING THE GAP
SUE MILLER

Glancing at the clock, he made one last quick check round, dried his cup and saucer and folded the tea towel neatly. He propped the note against the teapot on the kitchen worktop and, pulling the door firmly behind him, double locked it. If he hurried he would just make it.

When Tony reached the station he met the usual mixture of people jostling forward towards the train pulling into Newcastle Central. The platform was crowded with Friday afternoon travellers including the inevitable hen do en route to York or London. He glanced up and down as people formed queues at each of the train's doors. Ahead of him was a young girl, probably a student, chattering and laughing into her mobile. She was a mass of colour and textures and jangling jewellery, a bright scarf tied round her head like a bandana and trailing through auburn curls. Behind there stood a tired looking middle-aged woman, dragging a rather battered overnight case and holding a carrier bag bulging with magazines and soft mints. Next was a well dressed lady wearing heels and a tailored grey suit. She looked like she might belong in first class. Finally there was a man and woman in their forties, arm in arm and talking in soft tones as they leaned into each other. They kissed briefly as they waited their turn to climb inside and Tony averted his eyes. Their affection for each other seemed uncomplicated. He didn't need reminding that not everyone was that lucky.

For once, the train left the station on time. He sighed with relief. Perhaps things were finally looking up. Seat numbers were checked and luggage stowed as the train wound its way out of the station, crossed the river and started the run south. He could usually not get enough of this view up and down the river, bridges to east and west, bright light bouncing off the water, the sky stretching a clear canopy above. But today he had no time and was in no mood for sightseeing.

They sped through Gateshead without incident but when they reached Durham, the usual five minute stop soon stretched to ten. Then, just as irritation was building, the on board announcement system crackled into a life that belied the reassuring if world weary tones of the man in charge.

"This is your train manager, Gary Harrison. I am sorry to have to tell you that there has been an incident between Durham and Darlington. We are being held at Durham station till further notice. As soon as I have more information I will let you know."

Juggling case, bag, phone, laptop, Tony had looked for a seat near a working plug socket and, to his relief, found one and fired up his computer straight away. Now he groaned. This was all he needed. In that instant, being without access to the internet seemed the least of his worries. This had happened to him before. They might be stuck here for hours. Feeling beads of sweat forming on his forehead, he loosened his tie and undid the top button on his shirt. Life was complicated enough without any more drama. He just wanted to get to Darlington in one piece, get this presentation over and done with and life back on track. Was that too much to ask?

"I do apologise for any inconvenience this incident may cause. I have been informed that the air ambulance has arrived but I have no further information about the likely delay time. I would however like to advise you that Virgin trains do operate a compensation scheme."

There was much pushing and shoving. Fractious passengers arriving for what should have been the next train to leave Durham for London filled the vestibule spaces between the carriages or remained on the platform trying to gamble their options. A stuffy and heated air of stoic resilience settled over the seated travellers.

The young female student suddenly reappeared, having elbowed her way through the passengers standing next to the toilets, checking black bags on luggage racks as she worked her way along the carriage. She was speaking breathlessly into her mobile.

"Kelly, it's me, Gemma. I'm on the train and, oh my God, I've lost my laptop. It had all my photos on, my dissertation, everything. I just nipped to the loo for a second and left it on the seat and now the train's packed and it's gone. I don't know what to do."

Wild eyed and red faced, she looked like she was going to cry. A few heads turned, registering mild interest in her predicament but little else. No one moved. Gemma continued to make her way through the carriage, alternating between talking into her phone and asking anyone who would listen if they had seen a black laptop. Tony registered that each time she stretched to the luggage racks her jumper slid upwards, revealing just enough flesh to attract the attention of some of the men on board. She was however oblivious to their glances, far too focused on her search and she soon disappeared from view. Her progress however, if he'd bothered to look, could be measured by the dipping and bobbing of heads as she questioned everyone she passed.

"Ladies and gentlemen, this is your train manager speaking. If you have luggage on seats can you move it to the overhead racks to make

room for your fellow passengers joining the train. As soon as I have any more information about the delay I will let you know."

Tony was in an aisle seat and had put his bag deliberately on the chair next to him as if keeping it for someone, avoiding eye contact and continuing to punch information into his computer. His actions and attitude managed to create a virtual exclusion zone around him and every few minutes he ran his fingers through his hair till it spiked hedgehog-like. He pulled out a large crumpled handkerchief and mopped his brow. Taking a bottle of water from his bag, he gulped down its contents without tearing his eyes from the screen. The woman he'd thought belonged in first class was opposite, talking on her phone, oozing quiet efficiency. Unlike him, she seemed in control of her life. As he listened, he could feel jealousy making him start to hate her.

"Hi, Peter, I'm stuck at Durham. Yeah, sounds like someone's been hit on the line outside Darlington... Dunno, maybe... Anyway, could you get the washing out of the basket and stick it in the machine? Yeah, thanks, it's just I'm at work tomorrow and I need a clean blouse."

Eventually the train idled out of Durham. There wasn't much in the way of visible reaction, just a collective undramatic sigh of British understatement.

"Ladies and gentlemen, this is your delayed 15.46 Virgin train service to London King's Cross. We are running approximately sixty five minutes late due to an earlier incident. Estimated times into stations now are as follows..."

The weary looking middle-aged woman, Helen, was trying to read the copy of 'Hello' she'd bought from WH Smiths. She usually only glanced at it in the hairdressers but she always tried to mug up on celebrities before she saw Emma so she didn't look too ignorant when her daughter was filling her in on the latest soap star gossip. But she'd been distracted by the lost laptop drama. Poor girl, about Emma's age, she'd thought, though she couldn't ever imagine her Emma leaving a laptop unattended. Perhaps she'd better ring and tell her what was happening. Or it might be easier to avoid a scene and just send her a text. She already had the feeling this weekend was something of an inconvenience to her daughter; she was always so busy these days. She'd barely pushed the send button when her phone rang. It was Emma.

"I don't know what time I'll get in, dear... There's been some sort of incident with someone on the line... Well, yes, I can see it's annoying for you... Probably... they've sent for an air ambulance... I know, it might seem a bit selfish but I'm sure they didn't do it on purpose to annoy us... Perhaps whoever it was had other things on their mind... Anyway we'll still go out when I get there... yes, how's London? Thirty degrees, wow... well, yes, I suppose you're right,

should get my ticket money back at least... yes, I'll have some wine on the train."

Just outside Darlington they stopped again. This time they were in the middle of nowhere. From the window everything looked ripe. The colours were a kaleidoscope of greens and blues. Rooks whirled languidly above the tree tops preparing to roost for the night. It had rained hard for a couple of days and everything was bursting with steamy warmth. The air was sweet with the scent of damp grass and heavy with pollen. It was a perfect evening.

"Once again we apologise for the delay to your journey. This is due to an earlier incident just north of Darlington. We are now waiting for clearance so we can get you on your way."

The couple, Jenny and Craig, were seated across the aisle from Tony. He tried his best to ignore them but it was difficult, they seemed to more than fill their space and had spread themselves over most of the table. It was obvious that they had come well prepared for the journey and seemed to know how to have fun. They had littered the table with crisps, dips and half a dozen cans of lager. Jenny wrapped her arm round her partner's shoulders and snuggled into his side. Craig gave her leg a playful squeeze and then, looking out of the window, tapped his free hand on the table in frustration.

"What possesses people?"

"I know, love. But there's nothing we can do. Let's just enjoy ourselves. It's okay, we can go another time."

Ten minutes ticked by and then, with a jolt, they progressed at a snail's pace along smooth tracks. They passed a farmhouse, cows chewing grass, purple vetch glowing in the early evening sunshine. Weeds with golden daisy-like flowers bobbed their heads in the gentle breeze.

Then they went under a bridge.

Tony glanced up from his screen. The splash of colour struck him: bright orange glaring from the trackside. There were about eight men in total, all in high vis jackets huddled in various attitudes along the bank, picking over the scene, sombre. The train passed almost before he had time to register what was going on. And anyway, he wasn't connected. It wasn't like he and whoever had jumped had anything in common.

They came to houses, one or two at first and then as they went closer to the town, it was possible to see streets winding to the edge of estates in the distance. And they passed homes with gardens that ran down to the track. Jenny watched them fly by as she started to doze, hundreds of houses, thousands of tales. Craig had always wanted to travel and she'd been the one who'd not been too bothered and happy to stay at home. But she'd started to see the attraction in seizing the day and just going for it. Like he'd always said: you only get one go at this.

Helen's phone rang as they approached Darlington, and, with a sigh, she answered.

"Don't worry about me, Emma love, you just go ahead and have your tea and I'll get something when I get in. It's like a soap opera on this train. There's folk crying, people trying to get somewhere to sit, stuff going missing. You couldn't make it up."

And in an ordinary-looking house with a garden that ran down to the track on an ordinary estate where an ordinary father just hadn't been able to take it any longer, an ordinary little boy came home from school clutching his end of year report to find strangers in the kitchen, an open envelope on the table and his ordinary mum in tears.

"Where's Dad?"

It wasn't how summer holidays were supposed to start. She had tried to call her lover but she couldn't get through. He'd had to go to Darlington for a presentation.

"Ladies and gentlemen, this is your train manager Gary. In a few minutes time we will be arriving into Darlington station. We do apologise for the delay and hope this will not have caused you too much inconvenience. Please make sure you have all your possessions. We wish you a safe onward journey. And when alighting from the train, please mind the gap."

TO KING AND COUNTRY
DAVID A MURRAY

Face flushed with excitement the young boy ran into the living room. "Dad, dad, the Germans have shot Grandad Carter!"

His father smiled and turned away. Grandad hadn't even seen a German in fifty years.

"They have, I've really really seen it!"

"That was years ago, son. Now don't bother grandad. He's trying to get washed."

In the bathroom the old man struggled back into his shirt. It was getting harder every year. Glancing at the scar running almost the length of his back, he winced at a sudden pain. It was getting worse.

It hadn't hurt at all at first.

The memory of that night in Belgium, that night in no man's land outside of Passchendaele. It was as vivid now as it always had been.

He tried to shrug it off but couldn't. It was all a long time ago. What was the name of that sergeant again? Wilson, yes, that was it.

Memories and he was back again on Newcastle station on his way back to Belgium. He remembered he'd bought a paper and read the headlines. 'Third Ypres, Big Push on Passchendaele'.

It stopped him dead. His battalion had moved into that sector just before he'd left. He knew he'd be walking into hell.

When he first saw the sergeant, he was leaning on a girder, smoking. He nodded, "Wilson East Yorks." From the state of his uniform he was no stranger to the Western Front. He went on, "Seen the headlines, son? If they're planning a big push it means they've already started. Even our lot aren't dim enough to let them know what we're going to do before we do it. Bloody marvellous! Where's your mob at?"

"Ypres."

The other paused then blurted out, "I'm dead pissed off with it all."

"Aye, it only hurts when you laugh. Ever thought of not going back?"

"Hasn't everyone?"

"No, I mean it!"

The boy stopped dead. He didn't know whether the other was serious. They shot men for desertion. Afterwards, sitting together on the train, both seemed to consciously avoid the subject. It was only as the train pulled into King's Cross that the older man raised the question again. "Well, do we or don't we?"

Carter simply nodded, half hoping the sergeant had forgotten their earlier conversation. If things should go wrong he could always blame the older man.

"Good, I've an aunt in Neasden. She'll put us up for a few days. Uncle Ted was killed on the Marne and she hates the bloody army." He paused. "Mind, the second we leave the station, we'll be easy pickings. The place is lousy with MPs so watch it."

The man was right. King's Cross Station was alive with police – military and civilian – but there were so many soldiers milling around that they passed through unnoticed. Even the bus to Willesden was crowded and they were glad to get off.

"Where to now?" the boy queried.

"Other side of the park. By the way, the sooner we get rid of these uniforms the better. They're a dead giveaway!"

It was only then that the boy realised the seriousness of his position. Out of uniform and with an expired pass he could be shot.

He glanced down. It was the same filthy rag he'd been fighting in for nearly two years. It even had a smell of the trenches. He would gladly be rid of it even though chucking it could well mean a short and violent end to his military career in front of a firing squad.

As they neared the corner of Chapter Road and Willesden, Carter saw the MP. The man was half hidden in a shop doorway. Carter nudged Wilson violently and the pair lurched to a sudden halt.

Judging by the man's uniform he'd been no closer to the front than Southend Pier. Checking their passes he glared at Carter. "This expires in less than twenty four hours. How the hell do you expect to get back in that time?" he snapped peevishly.

Receiving no answer, he turned on Wilson. "And yours is just as bad. You should know better, sergeant. You know what they do to people like you over there!"

There was a stony silence.

"They're stood up against a wall and shot!" He paused. "Go back now and you might just get away with it and don't worry. I'll make sure you do go back!"

It was Hobson's Choice. The MP had their details and they'd be forwarded on.

It took a long time for the King's Cross bus to arrive. Neither spoke. Carter glanced up at the sky. He'd never seen it so blue.

He remembered the legless, armless, sightless wrecks he'd seen and the seemingly countless dead of both sides. They'd be a couple of lunatics returning to the asylum. He'd been slightly wounded twice already and resisted the thought of third time lucky; unless it was a Blighty one of course.

He'd still get out of it.

That thought stuck with him all the way back to France even when they were both incarcerated in the airless windowless box in the bowels of the ship which served as the brig.

Carter glanced across at Wilson and was struck by his seeming cheerfulness. Slouched against the bench that ran the length of the wall. He seemed a world away.

The young Carter had spent his whole life in Newcastle. He had a blurred memory of reporting to Fenham Barracks and of his brand new uniform of which he was so proud. Then of being taken south to Yorkshire, south of the river beyond Middlesbrough, which reminded him so much of Newcastle, to an army camp near the little village of Marske by the Sea. The local countryside entranced him. It was a different world to the crowded city streets of his hometown. What he wasn't to know was that crossing the Tees would eventually lead him into a world of horror which would haunt his nightmares for the rest of his life.

If he ever thought that France would simply be an extension of the early years then subsequent events would prove him shockingly wrong. He glanced down at the mud-stained shabby thing his uniform had become and grimaced. That brought him back to the cramped brig. As he looked back, it felt as though time telescoped in on itself. It seemed that one minute they were waiting for the ship and the next in front of the panel of officers then sentenced. One week's field punishment. Wilson lost his stripes.

Field punishment was brutal. Wilson knew that few survived it. Offenders were fastened to the wheels of an artillery piece for an hour at a time almost in full view of the front line and took part in the most dangerous missions.

Both were tied at the wrist and forced into a sitting position. It had rained for weeks and they found themselves in a shallow pool of very cold water. A movement caught the boy's eye and an enormous rat ran over his outstretched legs. They were everywhere.

The rain intensified. "Bit like an August bank holiday in Redcar," Wilson called out. Head hanging, rain streaming down his face, the boy didn't answer. His bleeding wrists hurt like hell and the thought that he'd never even been to Redcar came and went. Then he slumped forward semi-conscious. He was beginning not to care and started to shiver uncontrollably. Don't go to sleep, he heard himself whisper.

In spite of himself, he drifted off and was jerked awake by someone kicking his leg. "On your feet, you're going on a little trip." It was a senior NCO in the Border Regiment. "They need a prisoner and you and your mate are going over to get him. Don't worry, you won't be on your own. We've a bunch of other miscreants to go with you." He cut the ropes. "Now on your feet and get over to Lieutenant Forbes in Observation and be quick about it."

He turned to the other. "Hello Willy, hear you lost your stripes. You can have mine if you want, they're more trouble than they're worth." He laughed. "Hear you're going on a little trip. Maybe you'll cop a Blighty one." He paused. "Anyway, the best of luck. I'll save your place for you when you get back."

"Sod off!"

The NCO grinned. "You heard what I told your mate and careful when you stand up, you've been sitting there a long time and watch your young friend there, he looks done in!"

"Before you do sod off maybe you could tell me what this is all about."

"They're trying to take a little village called Passchendaele about two miles over there. We've already lost hundreds and they're still no nearer taking it."

Lieutenant Forbes was in the observation post. He was sitting behind a makeshift desk, up to his ankles in water, and in a foul mood.

"You've already been briefed. Wilson, I want you to be senior man. Remember, get a prisoner then straight back. Don't hang about!"

It was 4am and in spite of the dark they could still make out the dozens of dirty green pools that lay between them and the German lines. It had been raining for weeks.

They were not simply frightened. They felt something far beyond that.

"Good luck, Geordie," Wilson whispered. "See you back in the Boro."

Then they were sliding out over the sandbags, under the barbed wire, and out into the blackness of no man's land.

Suddenly he couldn't find Wilson and reaching out into the darkness, his hand touched a boot.

Please don't let this be what I think it is, he thought. But it was. The corpse of a long dead German soldier. He stopped and hugged the wet earth terrified.

"Will you get a bloody move on?" came a coarse whisper from behind. "We haven't got all bloody night!"

Away down the line the staccato rattle of a German machine gun broke the silences. Then it was quiet again.

He forced himself to crawl over the rotting corpse, gagging at the stench. He told himself that they couldn't be that far from the German lines now and that soon the nightmare would be over.

There was a muffled report ahead and Carter watched mesmerised as three tiny lights rose high above the German lines. They seemed to hang motionless for a second then exploded, flooding the whole area with a harsh white light. The whole patrol stood out like crows on a telegraph wire. Then the German line seemed to explode. The noise was deafening.

Carter turned and ran. Something struck him heavily in the back and he was suddenly face down in the mud. He arose with difficulty and, as he turned, he saw Wilson fall.

Then he was back in the British trench almost colliding with Lieutenant Forbes.

"I see you've buggered it up again!" he exclaimed testily. "And where the hell is Wilson?"

"I saw him go down, sir. So far as I know he's had it."

"Pity, cut along to the dressing station and get yourself seen to. You're bleeding like a stuck pig!"

"I'm alright, sir, I just fell over."

Forbes snorted. "And don't bloody argue. I've got enough to worry about. You've been hit, man, and badly by the look of it. If you don't believe me, feel for yourself."

Carter reached into the small of his back. It simply felt numb but when he took his hand away, it was bright with blood.

Still thinking he'd hardly been scratched, he carefully levered himself out of the trench and made his way toward the dressing station, a tiny dot far behind the lines. He was obviously bleeding but still couldn't feel anything though the numbness was beginning to wear off. Before he'd covered half the distance, he was in agony and barely able to walk. He passed out yards from the dressing station.

For a long time he knew nothing. There was a strange sense of movement, then the ship, and he remembered that only in fragments. He was only fully aware of his surroundings after he'd been in the British Military Hospital in Sheffield for the best part of a week.

Then he was back home on sick leave. The 'Big Push' was still on, with its inevitable sickening casualties. His back still hurt and he knew he'd been pushed out early to make way for the wounded who were pouring in. And they were sending him back.

Something like two months since he'd last stood there and he found himself on the same platform on Newcastle station waiting for the southbound train. The usual khaki-clad bustling crowd were milling around with the odd MP striving to maintain some kind of order, almost lost in the throng.

Stuff 'em all, he thought. For two pins I wouldn't go back.

Then interrupting the thought with an ear-splitting roar, and in a cloud of steam, the train was there. He forced himself aboard, shouldering his way along the crowded corridor.

Glancing out of the window he saw a man standing on the platform staring up at him. He was in civvies and for one unbelievable instant Carter thought he recognised Wilson. As they slowly moved out of the station, he looked again and imagined the beginnings of a sardonic smile. As the train gathered speed, he turned away then looked again but the man, whoever he was, was lost amongst the crowd. Then he was gone.

JIMMY JESUS
PAUL O'NEILL

1. When the river outlives its fish…

The shoes were the first thing I noticed. Shiny, black dress-shoes with a neat, white braiding, designed to glide across the parquet strips of a ballroom or perhaps to stand on the stage in a jazz club. In this case they were shuffling cautiously over the surface of the mud and had been twinned with a filthy pair of tracksuit bottoms. He approached slowly from my left-hand side, his movements having the shaky trepidation of the long-term drunk. I got the feeling at first that he probably wanted something from me. Maybe money or cigarettes or maybe something else.

He sat down with a sigh so that the two of us bookended the bench with the river, coffee-coloured, in front of us. For a time I pretended not to notice him.

I focused instead on the water that was ferrying objects like a conveyor from left to right: small tree-trunks, prams, carrier bags. I had been watching it for some time, trying to come up with an accurate word to describe its movement. I had decided that rolling wasn't the right word; I was almost certain at this stage that rolling was too strong a word, but there was strength in its movement and, just like the sea, you couldn't say with any conviction that it wasn't a living thing.

"You right there, pal?" he said. "You're no gaunny start crying ohn me?"

I kept my attention on the river. As he spoke I watched as the bodies of first my father and then my mother went floating by from left to right and then out of view.

I looked at him fully then for the first time. His skin was blistered with the weather and whatever else. A silvery line of mucus hung diagonally from his nose to his beard. He was a mess, I considered with all honesty, though his concern appeared to be genuine enough.

"I was just daydreaming," I said.

"Daydreaming, aye," he said. "And fucken crying."

"I wasn't planning on crying." Sometimes your own ears catch the sound of your own voice in the act of lying. I offered him a cigarette but he seemed to ignore the gesture. I looked back towards the river. By now, the bodies of various family pets were caught on the rocks in the centre, a pile of limp bodies and soaking wet fur. To put names to each of them would have been too painful and I knew, by instinct, that it was best not to look. When I re-opened my eyes, the force of the water had freed them. I watched as the current carried them towards the bend in the river, beneath the obscene word painted on the footbridge.

"Good," he said, "you see some jack sat crying ohn a bench. Go an ask if he's right and 'fore long there's two o ye's sat bawlin ohn a bench aside each other." He made a gesture with his knuckles as though he was wiping tears away from his eyes. "Now gie us one o them tabs, son, Chrissakes."

2. Every drop of water…

I looked down at the clothes I was wearing. My own black shoes were caked in the light-grey mud from the river bank. There were a number of splashes, the same colour, up the legs of my trousers.

"I take it you're no from round here, son," he said with the cigarette hanging from the side of his mouth. "It's a quare place te come for your hols. Specially dressed like that."

"I do come from here originally," I said. "Stockton. I've been living away."

"Right enough," he said.

"How about you?"

"Jes washed up here," he said, "two years, three years." He then straightened himself up. "Jamesie," he said, and held his hand out for me to shake. His hands were filthy, the fingers stained black and yellow, with long sharp nails like claws at the end.

"Patrick," I said.

"And is this your usual gehtup, Patrick?" he said, pointing towards my suit.

"I've come straight from church."

"Religious man?" he said, eyebrows raised.

"Funeral," I said.

"Right enough," he said and then fell silent in his own actions. He took a large plastic bottle from one of the bags he had with him. He then fished around in a second cloth bag and took out two metal cups, the type that double up as the lids of flasks. He held the bottle up to the light as if to check the clarity of the contents and then unscrewed the lid. His hands were shaking as he poured but he did a reasonable job and continued to pour until both cups were full. I watched as he screwed the lid back onto the bottle; I marked the ritual and the concentration in his actions. He handed one of the cups to me without speaking and then raised his own in the air.

"To the living," he said, coughing, "and the dead." He then raised his cup even higher, spilling dark brown liquid over the rim and onto the tops of his shoes.

"To the living and the dead," I said. We clinked our cups in the middle of the bench.

"And may the two sides..." he said, but before he finished his sentence he made a wheezing sound, a little like laughter, which then developed, gradually, into a fit of coughing.

"Sorry, son," he said, the cough taking hold.

I looked on, waiting for it to stop, unsure of what to do. At times the noise was low and guttural, and at other times high and wheezy, punctuated with swear words. The jerking of his shoulders made him spill more of his drink over the tops of his shoes. I took the cup from his hands and placed it on the ground beside him. After a time I sensed that he was struggling even to breathe and I wondered if I needed to hit him on the back or to move him into some kind of recovery position. His cheeks stood bright red against the yellow around his eyes.

"Are you going to be okay, Jamesie?" I said.

He made a series of 'f' sounds as though he wasn't able to finish the word. His hollow chest rattled once more.

"Jamesie," I said.

"Fine," he said, at last, his hand out in front of him.

I wasn't sure if he wanted me to take hold of his hand. I picked up his cup and placed it in his fingers.

"Good man, Patrick," he said, at last, and spat on the ground. "Pologies for all tha. A right old jess you'll think ah am."

The two of us then were silent for some time; Jamesie catching his breath, me watching the steady progress of the river. We smoked and watched the clouds of gnats hovering in the shadows of the bushes. All the time, the river continued its movement, at odds with the relative calmness of the day. I imagined the engines of some vast pump house at work further up the river, just out of view.

For some time the water had been ferrying sodden

pieces of paper and cardboard which I now recognised to be the books I had studied in school. These were followed by a number of plastic toys that I vaguely remembered playing with over the years of my childhood. With the minimum of fuss and without a single word spoken, Jamesie filled up the two cups once more. The sound of liquid hitting the cup, high and musical.

"This should help, son," he said. "I should know. Helps with all kinds of things."

The sun, by now, was on its way down, illuminating the hills in the distance with a soft orange glow. I took off my tie and pushed it into the pocket of my jacket. I undid the top two buttons of my shirt and got to thinking about the funeral.

The priest's words had seemed contrived at first, delivered in a tone which caused them to float and to drift in the vast space above our heads. In the pews beside me had stood a handful of my relatives, grown older, heads down, each one lost in their own collection of memories. Then the priest put together some words which seemed to resonate and to collectively shake us from our thoughts.

"I'm not a scientific man by any means," he had said, "but I recently heard two facts that I'd like to share with you, if I may. The first fact," he said, taking out a sheet of paper, "is that the human body is typically made up of around sixty percent water. This, of course, is reasonably well known. The second fact," he said, turning the paper over, "is that every single drop of water has been on this planet since the very beginning of time." He paused after this and I had looked around at the faces of my relatives, crying, blowing into their handkerchiefs.

3. O ye of little faith…

The phone in my jacket pocket was switched to silent but I had felt the vibrations of several missed calls. By now they would be looking to take the cling-film off the sandwiches. They'd be wondering where I was.

"Do you have any family, Jamesie?"

He shook his head and took a long drink from his cup. "Ask me another one," he said.

"Sorry," I said, "I don't mean to pry."

"You work away, son. You cannae keep too many secrets about yourself when your sleep'n at the back of Sainsbury."

"I suppose not," I said, "but I understand if you don't want to tell your story."

"See, Patrick," he said, "I always preferred a wee song over a long story." He looked straight ahead and the lines on his forehead moved closer together. For a moment I thought he was readying to sing a song. He made a small cough as though to clear his throat. I waited and remained quiet for a time. I watched the river and waited but no song came.

"Do you believe in God, Jamesie?" I said.

"Do and ah don't," he said after a long time considering the question. "Jes depends on when y'ask. There's plenty says ah look like the man above."

"The hair and the beard," I said.

"Jimmy Jesus the wee bastards call us. Throw'n stones from across the bank. But see," he said and leaned in towards me so that I got a blast of the spirits contained in his breath. His eyes were wide and he focused them directly on mine. "Hist'ries gaunny prove us right in the end, Patrick. One o these days ah'll get up and fucken walk across the top o that river and bray one of the wee shites. Ah'm the closest thing to a Saint this place has got." The last few words were coughed rather than spoken and he then descended into another, less violent, fit of coughing.

As he coughed, I pictured Jamesie standing up and taking slow, careful strides across the surface of the river. The clouds had separated sufficiently for the light to shine through and to offer a direct route from one bank to the other. On the opposite bank, the children dropped their bikes by their sides and looked on in disbelief. He held his arms out at either side, an orange carrier bag of cans and bottles hanging from the fingers of each hand. His fancy shoes made one unsteady step and then another, the weight being enough only to cause the slightest indentation on the surface of the river. Like a water-spider skating across a duck pond.

4. To swim and swim back…

"Will you stay here for good, Jamesie?"

"It's a good enough spot," he said, "few fellas sitting by their rods in the summertime. When the graft was here," he said, "the fesh all swam oaf. Then the work dried up and the fesh came back." He held his finger up in the air to make his point. "Ah'll tell you this, Patrick. It doesnae matter how hungry I got," he said, "you wouldnae catch me eating one."

I pictured Jamesie stripped to the waist, standing in the river with the sun beating down. The clouds in the sky were the dramatic, unbelievable kind from an old religious painting. Greys and blues and hints of pink. Scores of people watch from either bank as a child is passed along a human chain which ends at Jamesie. He takes the child, a boy, and first uses his cupped hand to trickle a small amount of water over his face. The boy begins to cry and to struggle as Jamesie pushes him on his back under the water.

"Ah'll stay jest as long as ah fancy," he said, "then ah'll jump in and swim back up home to die."

5. No more songs about the sea…

Perhaps the rum was much stronger than I first thought because all of a sudden the notion came over me to paddle in the river and, before I could stop myself, I had walked over to the bank and sat down amongst the reeds. I took off my shoes and placed them on the grass behind me. I then rolled the sock from each of my feet and placed them inside my shoes. I looked around and could see Jamesie in the shadows on the bench with his eyes smiling and his mouth wide open. I could see he was drunk. I could say with all certainty he was rolling drunk.

"Crazy wee ratchet that y' are," he shouted.

I placed my feet into the water and the cold felt like two strong hands which seemed to grab hold of each foot. The sky was beginning to darken by the second and the darkness by now could not be stopped. Occasionally the black shape of a bird or a bat would flash by but too quickly for me to make out if it was real or imagined. On the grass of the opposite bank I could make out the silhouette of a group of children on bikes.

"Sing me a song, Jamesie," I said and moved my feet back and forth, feeling the water moving, filtering, between my fanned toes. On the bench behind me, Jamesie laughed, cleared the phlegm from his throat and began to sing.

BLUE BRIDGE CROSSING
JANET PHILO

I know! Okay! I feel bad enough already. Dad needs this job.

The trouble is, I can never find a way to say sorry as if I mean it. Mam always says, "Sorry's too easy." I would give her a cheeky hug. Sometimes that works. But we're in the middle of the river, on the bridge, surrounded. And her face says 'No'. She never did like a scene, but she surely knew how to make one!

No! The plastic's ripping! I've got hold of it as tight as I can. But it's stretching like treacle off a spoon. Cheap plastic lets me down. And now there's rusty fur spewing out of the gash. I need to get a grip, hold on tighter, stop the slipping.

Dad said we have to get it back before kick off.

Mam's turned her face away. She pretends to look at the river. Anything but look at me. That's what she does when the thing she really wants to say, or do, to me is so bad she can't even admit it to herself! I notice the grey roots and dark strands among her blonde hair. I wonder if she's noticed them, or if she just can't afford to get it sorted. Another stab of guilt. I see a lot of the back of her head these days.

It was the best birthday ever. Five a side at the rec next to our house. Dad was the ref. He enjoyed it, I could tell. For a few minutes, he lost the vacant, dead-eyed expression he's had ever since he's been at home all day. Mam made hot dogs. Brought them out at half time, with cans of coke. If he loses this match-day stewarding job now because of me…

Roary came out of our house, before the match, it was the best! No one had a clue it was dad! Well, not until Roary had to disappear and the referee came out five minutes later! He got a mate to rig up a couple of speakers with the anthem and everything.

We didn't mean any harm when we nicked his lager stash after the match. Well I'm fifteen now. Your mates expect it. I'd have got all sorts of aggro from them if I hadn't. Wonder if dad was saving it to celebrate when he got a real job again?

It's only two hours to kick off. My feet and fingers are tapping now. I can't stop them. I'm losing it a bit! Wish I had a fag! Hope mam didn't hear that.

Mam cleaned Roary's head as best she could. She even sprayed it, made it smell nice. Well, made it smell a bit better anyway. They'll never notice, she reckons. She's ringing dad now. He'll meet us outside and take it in the back way. It has to be hanging up before Roary comes to get ready.

Oh please no! Not now! It's Tess. I didn't see her get on. She's by herself. I don't need this right now. What if she comes up to me? Time to take in the river view myself. 'Tess', nice name. She plays in goal for the girls' team. She's proper fit and she talks to me a bit. And now I'm standing here with the fur of a giant teddy poking out of rips in a plastic sack.

Derren Brown plays these mind games. You can make people believe whatever you want. Okay, I need to work hard on her mind. This is the giant teddy I've spent all my money on for my little sister's birthday. Dad says women like a 'new man', not afraid to show his sensitive side.

She's coming over. I didn't mean to actually encourage her, Derren! I wonder how cold the water is. I can't swim and Tess is next to me. I'm relying on you now, Derren. Or, do we go with 'Truth'? It's always best in the end! Mam says that, when she knows I'm not telling it exactly as it is. How do they know? Mams? No matter how hard you try, they just know.

So. Here goes. Speak to the river not her, that's got to be easier.

"Hi Tess! You off to the match?"

"Yeah, got my dad's season ticket, he couldn't come. You?"

My dad's a steward (as if that somehow explains things). I've got Roary's head in here. Don't worry, we'll get it back before the match starts. I threw up in it. Mam's cleaned it up and she says they'll never know. Can't disappoint the kids, can you?

"You are so disgusting!" She crinkles her face as she smiles, not exactly at me, but I'll take it anyway.

"So who's that then? She seems nice." Mam can't help herself, and treats me to the full-faced truth gaze as we walk towards the ground. I'm turning away now, watching Tess's hair lift in the breeze from the river.

WATER UNDER THE BRIDGE
ALAN PILKINGTON

"*Delays southbound over the Tees flyover,*" the traffic guy on the local radio cheerfully announced.

Bob didn't need to be told that; he could see for himself the brake lights ahead that indicated a familiar crawl over the river was in prospect. He turned off the radio and slowed to join the back of the queue.

A chance to look around and take in the lovely scenery, he thought, catching his own wry grin in the mirror. Ahead to left, the sprawling old ICI estate lay largely inert with some new businesses trying to reignite the area with 'renewables', 'recyclables' and probably some other 'ables' he'd never heard of, while over to the right the prison sat stark behind its sandstone walls.

He wondered how Charlie was getting on in there, banged up somewhat late in the day after getting away with a life of petty crime that had begun, as had his own, not far from here. They had both lived in Stockton, gone to school together, teamed up with a couple of other lads, Gerry Docherty and Walter Brown, to form a fearless foursome.

They had got into some sticky situations then. Gerry was always the leader, planning the scrapes and allocating the blame later. Charlie and Bob were the willing foot soldiers, accepting the roles given and enjoying their share of the spoils – apples scrumped from back gardens, pornographic mags nicked from the newsagent's, and underage alcohol bought from dodgy off-licences. Walter was different, always half disputing Gerry's authority without ever being able to impose his own. He would settle sullenly into a sort of deputy role providing unnecessary supervision of Bob and Charlie.

The queue began to shunt forward and looking straight ahead his gaze shifted to the pleasanter prospect of the distant Cleveland Hills, the pimple of Roseberry Topping a reminder of a first visit there, a class trip at the start of secondary school.

That was when Mary had arrived on the scene – knee socks, short skirt and a ribbon in her hair. Gerry had honed in on her as soon as the coach emptied its ragamuffin cargo by the roadside at Gribdale Gate. By the time the packed lunches had been demolished, they were chatting. On the journey back Gerry installed himself next to Mary, the void he left next to Walter filled unwillingly by a plain and overweight girl he'd evicted. For both her and

Walter the arrangement was less of an opportunity than an embarrassment.

From that day on, Mary was always Gerry's Mary, an adornment that added to his status throughout school till the day they all left with barely an O-level between them.

That outcome hadn't bothered Gerry. His old man ran a builders' yard and Gerry, smart enough where it mattered, with ready access to equipment, materials and contacts, soon carved out a construction business of his own. It was inevitable Charlie and Bob would end up working for him.

It was a few months after that Walter joined the firm, slipping into his old role in the gang, not a mere grafter like Bob and Charlie, but not quite 'management' either. Mind you, Gerry didn't really do management, he ran things single handed with some support in the office from Mary. Yes, Mary was still Gerry's Mary, at work and at home.

Through school Walter had steered clear of Mary, never quite forgiving her for chipping into the group. The closer she came to Gerry, the further the rest of them were distanced. Not a problem for Bob and Charlie; the intimate services she provided were not ones they could or would wish to perform. Nevertheless Walter resented her and remained cool when their paths crossed at work.

It started to change as the business grew and Walter was needed more and more to supervise jobs, deal with clients and take on more of the admin work. Maybe it was seeing Mary more as herself than an adjunct to Gerry that made the difference. Walter became attentive to her needs – a door opened here, a file passed over there. With Gerry spending increasing time on a new sideline in pubs, clubs and gambling, Walter found himself often called on to pick up Mary and drive her to some social engagement, or take her home when she had had enough.

Bob could see the signs, so could Charlie, they both knew the way the wind was blowing. They'd smirk about Gerry's blindness, speculate on Walter's inevitable come-uppance, wonder whether Mary would emerge stainless or tainted.

But Gerry trusted Mary and he trusted that Walter knew the consequences of any trespass onto his property.

Then one Monday morning, it was just Gerry in the office. He said Mary had gone to her mother's in York; as for Walter, he was 'away'. Speculation was rife; his two trusted lieutenants absent at the same time. Some reckoned they'd run off to Spain together, some reckoned Spain would not be far enough.

Or it could have been just coincidence; like the call Charlie and Bob had received over the weekend.

They were in the middle of a job laying concrete foundations for a slip road for the A19 flyover. When they got the call from Gerry on Sunday night to turn in early at the slip-road site, they did; and as trusted friends and employees laid the concrete as instructed before the rest of the gang arrived.

It was a week before Mary reappeared in the office,

subdued but with a slight tan. Of Walter no more was ever heard. A missing person that no one missed.

They had never discussed the overtime, or the generous cash bonus they received from Gerry. In time it was all just water under the bridge, or as one of them would say in the pub after a few pints, holding the other's eye with a meaningful, regretful, trusting gaze, just Walter under the bridge.

But Walter's disappearance seemed to change things. Bob got out of the firm early, drifted from job to job before landing this one. Not to everyone's taste, driving for an undertaker, but it suited him well enough.

At least it meant he was used to driving this slowly. Though it was ironic that this morning despite being in the van (the 'meat wagon' as they called it), he still couldn't put his foot down because of this traffic; he could have walked the flyover quicker.

Inching forward, the water was below him now, Charlie's prison still showing in his wing mirror. Charlie had stayed with Gerry's firm as the legitimate business slumped to be replaced by corruption and crime, and the law had finally caught up with him. Mary had seen the light a while since and gone off to Spain for good, leaving Gerry to his decline through gambling and bankruptcy to smoking – and drinking – induced ill health. It was surprising he had lasted this long really.

And now here Gerry was in the back, slowly crossing the river as part of his final journey, via the Chapel of Rest, to the crem. Would Mary be at the funeral? Was she even alive? If she was, would she even know or care about Gerry kicking the bucket?

Although that reunion seemed unlikely (even more water under that bridge), it struck him that, here and now, the four lads had at least been brought back together by this bumper to bumper crossing of the Tees. He had Gerry in the back, Charlie over in the prison, and Walter, in all probability, under the bridge.

ICE CREAM TEES
KELLY ROSE

Leo heard him before he saw him. His arch rival was one of the modern breed of van men who played Rihanna and Ed Sheeran tunes where Leo still pootled about to the tune of Twinkle Twinkle. It really didn't work in his opinion. Even a brand new sound system couldn't cope with a modern tune, and the overall effect just sounded weird. He wondered if it was bitterness talking because this guy (if it was indeed the same guy and not an array of basic wage temp workers) was consuming his business week by week. Something was going to have to be done soon, otherwise Leo would himself be joining the zero contract brigades.

"So, is your name really Leonardo?"

It took Leo a few moments to locate the owner of the disembodied voice. This was in part because it measured not quite four feet in height but also because it involved him doing a painful manoeuvre over the hard Formica counter. It was also clad in more wool than your average Welsh Mountain Sheep, which had the overall effect of muffling her speech.

"Nah," he sighed, "so you know the Italians are the forefathers of ice cream production? I just pretend I have Italian roots for business purposes…"

He stopped short. 'The voice' probably wouldn't understand.

"What roots… like a tree you mean?" it piped by way of a response.

Despite the conversation being hard work, and with his week's poor sales still lodged in the back recesses of his mind, Leo couldn't help but chuckle.

"No lass, not those kinds of roots… well, maybe, sort of…"

He realised he was starting to flounder. But 'the voice' never paused for clarification. It simply extended a tiny fist towards his nose, unfurling the fingers one by one to reveal tarnished pearly pink nail polish and a fifty pence piece.

"I'll have whatever that will get me," she instructed.

Leo sighed again. Even his cheapest cone was at least three times the price but he still swivelled around to fill a double.

"I suppose you'll be wanting strawberry glitter on that, and chocolate dusting?"

"If it's included in the price," was the thrifty reply.

"Aye, pet, it's included."

He handed over the ice cream with as much ceremony as he could muster. The voice beamed and skipped briskly away, managing somehow to negotiate the double cone all the while yelling something about telling her nana all about him. Leo's heart sank. Oh dear, he thought to himself, I'm in trouble now.

Leo cast about him and, sensing the little girl to be his only clientele, made ready to move on, following a careful procedure he must have carried out a thousand times. He knew through painful experience that an emergency stop could result in close to a week's loss of earnings. Plus, what with it being February, the roads could be perilous.

Mooching along the deserted Saltburn streets caused Leo to overthink the grand scheme of life. Certainly, he had never set out to sell ice cream but like so many episodes it somehow seemed to evolve without his agreement. So now he dished out all kinds of dessert combinations to the good people of this seaside town come rain (last estimate, 67% of the time) or shine (a paltry 8%!). He couldn't say it was all bad. He liked the variety of characters it exposed him to, although the tourists were generally easier to please than the locals. The latter had been known to sometimes give him grief because they knew where to find him.

Of course folks assumed his days were filled with one long continuous bask in the sunshine, dishing out joy. He had realised long ago it wasn't their fault as their vision of his life was a bit like a good photo, squared off in the view finder, cutting out all the less attractive edging. Many were on holiday, looking at the sea, full of serotonin, eating his delicious ice cream. How could they possibly imagine his struggles?

The reality had even secretly inspired the name of his latest ice cream flavour. He had called it 'The Passion Biter'. It was especially popular with the ladies. The buying of a scoop would illicit more sniggers than any other, a classic mix, he thought, of indulgence and innuendo. Little did they know the actual cynicism upon which the title was founded!

Then again would they even care? Saltburn town was all about pleasure and escapism. It caused many folks to cast aside their usual empathy or charity. Traits that governed their daily lives were packed away like winter woollies, to be taken out of the cupboard when they returned home. This had been the inspiration behind the naming of his uniquely coloured 'Escapism' variety. He'd used a blue food dye for it which had resulted in an azure creation, like eating a slice of sky, he often thought.

Indeed, Leo liked playing with colours. 'Tempt a Turtle' was vibrant green, 'Ionian Sundae', a peachy rose. He also tried humour. 'Sun and Slaughter' was his new take on raspberry ripple, and his own personal favourite. For Leo, things were very much about the present. Maybe that explained why he seemed to have an affinity and understanding of ice cream, a substance that demanded focus completely on the moment, or risk losing the full quota of pleasure.

Maybe that also explained why he was newly single,

soon to be divorced, and continually criticised by his ex-wife for his lack of foresight and his constant failure to water and keep alive her extensive range of house plants!

And it wasn't just Mira who pushed the point home. His best mate, Tom, (class of '85's 'High Achiever') was never slow in offering his take on Leo's failures in life. Afterwards, he had 'played' at being mean but Leo knew he was a good guy inherently, so all this hurt like hell. Was the solution to simply become uncaring and ruthless, which had never been part of his make-up? His father used to joke he'd drive an extra mile to avoid a slug crossing a wet street. But as things had got worse during the last few months he had begun to wonder if they all had a point.

Ares never understood the term 'zero contract' when he was taken on. Governed by a life of rules, he had incorrectly assumed it correlated to some kind of freedom. The other lads soon filled him in.

"Just means you got no rights, mate," they chorused.

He was in no position to barter, so glumly accepted the news. The phrase "At least I have a job" became the most frequently played in his mind. His wife, even with limited English, also quoted it too.

"Xéro agápi, xéro," he would automatically reply in his native tongue, "I know, love, I know."

He had spent over eighteen months trying to find employment so when he finally landed this job, he grabbed hold as his entire livelihood, and new start in the UK, was at stake. The company boss was a ruthless entrepreneur, solely fixated on the ballooning dimensions of his own bank balance. He took full advantage of ensuring his employees' rights ran at a minimum.

Moreover, Ares was instructed to ignore a code of ethics that made him more than uncomfortable, almost nauseous. He had to purposefully poach on another's established turf. He'd been second guessing the blue and cream van's route now for over six months, and he was good at it. He also had to subtly insinuate his competitor's health and safety breaches such as the use of rancid base ingredients, cockroach infested cupboards and lack of any hygiene. The fact that the little van gleamed, daily radiating old world charm never failed to impress him, and it was such discrepancies that caused him sleepless nights. The plain truth was, he admired this man without question.

A few days later and 'the voice' was back. The first Leo knew about it was a blur of a slightly battered, too small bike coming to an emergency stop outside the counter window, swiftly followed by an unceremonious 'parking' on the kerb, in such a manner that more than explained its current state.

"Follows me, will ya?" the heavily coated little girl demanded. And with that she was re-mounted in a second and already at the bend, pausing briefly to beckon him again to hastily bring up the rear.

Flabbergasted, Leo wondered if there was some kind

of emergency, perhaps her nana was in trouble? He really felt he had little alternative but to do as she bid. So he revved up the engine and reversed. She was waiting for him just around the corner. They negotiated several streets together before stopping outside a gabled affair on a wide avenue. It wasn't just the faint cabbagey aroma emanating from the place that convinced him it was an old folk's home; there were three mobility scooters out front and a tired looking sign losing its battle with some ivy which announced it to be 'New Horizons Retirement Care Home'.

He parked the van in the forecourt and entered the gloomy foyer feeling more than a little uncomfortable. A young but fierce receptionist, busy pestering her cuticles, looked up. "Can I help you?" she barked with a look that suggested goodwill did not come naturally.

He found himself momentarily lost for words. The sentence 'a little girl asked me to follow her' really wouldn't go down well! "Err... I'm the ice cream man," was his eventual opener. And it worked like a dream.

The scowl was replaced by a Cheshire Cat grin, the fingernails abandoned and a sudden radiance melted all former hostility in an instant.

"Ahh yes, Penny had mentioned she was off to fetch you."

"Yes, I followed her straight in. My van is just outside," he added rather pointlessly.

"Well, in that case, I shall rally the troops," she beamed.

Stationed back inside the van's interior, Leo heard a bell

tolling deep in the bowels of the home somewhere and all of a sudden elderly folks poured from every orifice of the buildings, fifty arthritic fists clutching crisp, five pound notes. A few ambled unaccompanied but most came with all manner of frames, canes and mobility aides. Others were chaperoned with visitors and relatives, and the last group stayed fixed in their chairs gesticulating wildly to a nominee their flavour preferences. Five minutes later and Leo was actually breaking into a physical sweat to keep pace with the orders.

And thirty minutes later he had nearly sold out of both his Madagascan Vanilla Pod and Toffee Deluxe creams. But this half hour is all it took for the germ of a genius idea to be sewn. Leo just couldn't understand why he'd not thought of it before. Clearly, turning geriatric didn't diminish appreciation for all things ice cream.

As the queue finally began to peter out, Leo spied the diminutive figure of the voice.

"It's Penny, isn't it?" he enquired.

"Ma always calls me Penelope," she groaned, "but my mates just call me Tiny."

"Well, young lady, you have just earned yourself free cones forever as a thank you for throwing me a lifeline."

"Wot, like a life guard?"

"Yes, a champion one, Penelope!"

"Glad to have been of service," she said, whilst executing a mock curtsy at the same time.

Leo got the feeling she was a whole lot smarter than she let on.

"My nana says your cone was better than the cream teas they usually serve on an afternoon, cos the scones just end up clogging her false teef something awful."

Leo couldn't help but laugh out loud at that image. "No more denture fears, Leo's smooth ices are here!" he trilled. Not a bad jingle, he decided to himself…

During this short time it had struck him, the old, like the young, never lost their love of simple pleasures such as ice cream. With the umpteen care homes in Saltburn, he quickly formulated a plan. He could make good here, maybe even expand?

Ares killed the speakers in order to follow the blue and cream van at a safe distance. Today though it had suddenly veered from its normal route, diverting instead down a wide, tree lined avenue populated with sprawling detached properties each with formidable boundaries. His curiosity spiked and he parked up just out of sight on the opposite side of the road, leaning eagerly forward in his seat to marvel at the scene playing out before him. A snake-like stream of very old people poured forth from the building decked out in a colourful array of winter clothes, seemingly delighted in their brief exposure to the crisp but bitter air. They patiently waited in the queues for their turn to order but each came away in a childlike ecstasy, clutching all manner of delights. Within moments, some had dribbled huge globs of pale, soft ice cream over scarves wound tight around their necks, whilst others stabbed ferociously at small tubs of more solid sorbets and sundaes. Then there were those chomping rather unsuccessfully at flakes, leaving large chocolate shards down coated fronts. One even brandished a vibrantly wrapped ice pop like they'd just found a prize winning lottery ticket.

Ares felt inspired, elated for the guy and also made an uncharacteristically bold decision there and then.

As Leo turned to leave, he spied the single figure loitering near his van, hopping about nervously like he had been caught short of a handy WC. Wiping his still sweaty brow, he re-entered the van from the rear and put on his customer smile at the hatch. The guy who stood before him had a swarthy complexion that clearly delineated his foreignness. This was confirmed when he put in a heavily accented request for "…one large Ionian Sundae, please… and a job."

GHOST BRIDGE
JACQUELINE SAVILLE

It was the farm cats that sensed it first, though all morning the hairs on my arms and the back of my neck had been raised like antennae picking up faint signals of the uncanny. When the TV archaeologists had trekked north, tramped around, and traipsed across the riverbed it seemed they had stirred up more than silt and ancient timbers.

"What's up, mog?"

The world hadn't got so out of kilter that I expected an answer, but the sound of my voice was reassuring. Or it was to me – the cat was still poised to flee with its ears back, watching something I couldn't see. I crouched beside it and it bolted back up the field, swirling the air around my head and sending me the scent of horses. I told myself I must have just missed the trespassing riders, cutting through the field again and upsetting the cat who wasn't used to them. Then I heard the jingling of harnesses coming up from the river's edge, drawing nearer with the clop of hooves on a hard surface that didn't exist.

By the time my sister turned up half an hour later I could see hazy outlines, hear snatches of a language I couldn't understand. I could smell unwashed bodies and damp wool.

"What's up with you?" she said.

My mouth was probably hanging open. I was certainly sat in a field staring.

"Can you not see them, Annie?"

"See what?" she said, sitting cross-legged next to me. "Jeez, is that you?"

Annie got the smell first, muffled sounds soon after, same as I had earlier.

"What the…?" She linked her arm in mine and leaned closer. "It's like there's people, loads of people."

"Roman soldiers, I think," I said. "Coming up Dere Street on the way to the wall."

We could hear the drumming of marching feet on a wooden bridge we couldn't yet see. The men materialised as they moved up the slope, and passed us.

"They're not turning off into the fort," Annie said.

"Maybe for them it doesn't exist yet."

Before the week was out, everyone in Piercebridge had seen or heard or smelt the ethereal legions. Some of us started to recognise sections of the march, as though this was a film clip playing on repeat. It seemed weird but harmless until a couple of teenagers dared each other to race across the wooden bridge. Thankfully the water wasn't deep and the worst they got was bruises and a chill.

"We can't go on like this," Annie said. "What if a tourist sees them and crashes their car or walks down a road that isn't there?"

"What do you suggest?" I asked her, but I'd already had an idea of my own.

In waders, in shorts with bare feet, in swimming costumes, the town gathered at the edge of the Tees. Some thought I was barmy, but they were all more willing to listen than they would have been before our insubstantial visitors. We stepped into the water, each carrying something we'd be sore to lose, and lined up either side of the wooden bridge that most of us could see, though none could feel.

My dad started us off, throwing his best reading glasses into the water with the quiet splash of a fish breaking the surface.

"Shouldn't we say something?" Annie said, but it was too late for that. Everything from coiled rope to cooking utensils, high-heeled shoes to phone chargers was plopping and kersplunking into the river.

"Quiet, isn't it?" I said into the breath-held silence that followed, piercing the awestruck atmosphere.

Over the next couple of weeks I saw friends and neighbours down the bottom of the field in ones and twos, watching the water. They nodded when they saw me and I never asked them if they too heard the distant sound of sandals. The bridge has faded back into obscurity, but on still mornings I stand in the field with my eyes closed and let the wisps of horse-scent seek me out.

GRAPHITE
DAVID SMITH

I bet if I scratched around the bollards, poked into the old sleepers, I would find traces of it. The dockers cursed the arrival of the SS Conway from India that sullen November with her 1000 tonnes of it. Because it got everywhere, down your neck, in your hair and ears, so off-loading was very sulky. It would not have been the best time to tell them that graphite takes its name from ypaQo (grapho) Greek for 'to draw or write'. No, not a good time at all.

Taken into a corner, Bill Thompson, the foreman docker, whispered that he was going to the night match, to his sacred place, Ayresome Park. There on the green velvet moorland baize, he was convinced that Dicky Robinson would stop the great white stag from Leeds, John Charles, with his impeccable sliding tackle. Then his promise, "I've told this lot to get that last wagon loaded before I come back or there will be a row."

Twenty minutes into the game, the floodlights failed, plunging Bill into a graphite hole of despair, match abandoned.

So when I plug in the Temenos earphones I can still hear the tsunami of invective when Bill wrenched open the dock cabin door. I can see the scramble of men past his massive frame, the spilling of playing cards, newspapers, the crashing of chairs, as they stumbled back down the hold and the waiting penance of sow-like sacks.

Now, I stand in wonder and think of Anish Kapoor finding his way from India to this same blessed spot and with his graphite nib delineating the first sketches of his Temenos.

WATER UNDER THE BRIDGE
ALAN THEAKSTON

For once I had to put the alarm clock on. It's rare nowadays for me to have to catch anything as early as the six thirty out of Darlington station but, yesterday, I had to be in an office in the Euston Road by quarter past nine so didn't really have much choice. The older I get, and sixty seven is getting on a bit, the more comfortable my bed becomes and particularly so on a damp, misty and miserable October morning. It hadn't helped that I'd been at a business awards event until midnight the night before and although I'd only had three or four pints of beer and a glass of wine over the course of the evening, I had a slightly hungover feeling and was very tired.

I'd driven to the station from my home in the west end of Darlington and parked in the car park at the top of Victoria Road. I picked up a free copy of the Metro, queued for an Americano at the Costa outlet, walked through the unattended ticket gates and a few minutes later I was sitting comfortably in the first class carriage on platform one. I wasn't particularly looking forward to the day ahead, it was a long way to go just to tell people that they were about to become unemployed. As a director of a national company whose head office was in Middlesbrough, my task was to close down a subsidiary which was a minor part of a group of companies that we had acquired in the south. As part of the closure I had to lay off, or fire in other words, all thirty or forty employees. Not a particularly pleasant job but someone had to do it and I'd personally overseen many other similar closures before. The business was outdated and it was most unlikely that the employees, most of whom had been there for years, would be able to find new employment, but that was their problem, not mine.

As it was an early train I'd managed to get an empty table that seated four. I put my coffee down and emptied my pockets, putting glasses, tickets, wallet and phone on the table in front of me then took off my coat and jacket and laid them on the overhead rack. I plugged my laptop into the wall socket, brought up a spreadsheet on the screen and read the names of those about to lose their jobs. None of them meant anything to me, they were just employees who I'd meet once, give them bad news and never see again.

As we rattled past Rockcliffe Hall and on towards the railway bridge over the Tees at Croft, I looked around with that uneasy feeling that something wasn't right with the train. Not an entirely new feeling, I'd travelled on this route too many times before. It should be picking up speed on this stretch not losing it and as I sat wondering what had gone wrong it started jerking and slowing down before shuddering to a halt halfway across the bridge with the Tees flowing effortlessly below it. Great! I would have particularly little time to spare this morning and not for the first time my plans were disrupted by whichever rail company – currently Virgin but several over the last couple of decades – operated the East Coast Line. There was no point getting stressed, there was nothing I could do, I closed the laptop lid, took a sip of coffee and gazed out of the window into the gloom.

In my business life I'd taken this journey so many times over the last thirty years and yet this tiny fraction of it, crossing the Tees, always had the same unsettling, nostalgic and slightly depressing effect on me. It never failed to take me back to my childhood days in the early sixties when, as young as thirteen, I would regularly fish on this stretch of the river which belonged to Thornaby Angling Club. It also reminded me of those days when I would hurry round my paper job on a Saturday morning, get the bus at the top of Victoria Road to the station and, instead of the Tees, take the 08.08 to Richmond to fish the Swale. In those days the train would stop at Croft, Eryholme, Moulton and Scorton before arriving at Catterick Bridge where we would get off. By then diesels had replaced the steam trains on the route but the carriages remained battered and homely and there, already waiting for me,

I'd meet at least one other school friend and sometimes as many as eight or nine and we'd mess around and try to outdo each other with the new plugs, spinners, floats and other bits of tackle that we'd bought from Cummins's in Coniscliffe Road or Elliot's in Duke Street – both long since gone. When we got off at Catterick Bridge we'd walk the best part of a mile to Brompton on Swale and spend the whole day fishing for trout or, depending on the time of year, grayling, barbel, dace and chub before packing up our rods in the late afternoon, retracing our steps and getting coffee and sandwiches at the Bungalow Café by the station before catching the next train. The only time that I can remember fishing less than a couple of hours was in the snowbound January of 1963 when the line froze in the rod rings and the river was largely covered in ice. We played hockey with branches and a block of ice on the frozen river for ages until a couple of us fell through and, freezing and wet, we had to catch an early bus home.

I must have been sitting for several minutes gazing absently out of the window and reliving those days, lost in the past as the memories of times long gone returned, when, through the mist and drizzle, I noticed an angler standing by what we all called the sandhole – a small inlet just downstream of the bridge. It was unusual for someone to be fishing so early in the day at this time of year and I rubbed the window and leaned forward to get a better view. The figure was unclear in the gloom but as I peered hard my eyes adjusted and I could make it out to be that of a young boy wearing a donkey jacket, jeans and wellies. Next to him was a pushbike and canvas haversack. In his hands he held an old bamboo rod which was bending under the weight of a fish and as I watched he drew a roach or possibly a chub into an ancient landing net. Everything about him seemed to have been frozen in time.

As I stared hard at the scene, totally transfixed, the boy knelt and gently put the fish back into the river, watched it swim away then very slowly turned his head and looked directly up at me. He looked neither to the right nor to the left. It was as though I was the only person on the train and he knew exactly where I would be. His eyes fixed on mine and I saw his face quite clearly. It made no sense at all. The boy was me. The boy was me when I was only fourteen years old when my whole life lay ahead, when the days were long and filled with careless expectation. When my life revolved around fishing and friends and I never gave growing older or even a career a second thought. But that was not the impression that this boy gave. His look was one of sadness and silent accusation that seemed to say that I had let him down, that he was disappointed with me. He looked vulnerable and hurt. His steady gaze silently questioned me. It was a searching look. It was as though he was trying to ask what I had done to him over the years, why had I changed so much, why had I left him behind.

The train jolted and startled me back into the present as the wheels turned slowly and the engine gathered power and we moved on. I turned round, straining to keep him in sight and as we inched forward he raised his arm and waved hesitantly as we headed for the Yorkshire side.

For the next ten minutes I sat in a trance – in a time zone of my own. We must have passed through Northallerton station but I never noticed it. I could think of nothing else but the boy and his unspoken questions – and I began to think.

When had I changed so much? Why had I left the boy that I was behind? Where had I lost him? When did the gentle, thoughtful and compassionate boy turn into the cynical, hardened adult and, more importantly, why? How could I possibly have grown up into a man that the boy disliked – that, I realised, I too disliked?

I tried to think of explanations. Was it the change of lifestyle as my twenties approached and I left my teenage years behind? Was it the drinking, the night clubs and the women? They certainly can't have helped. Was it selfish ambition – the striving for recognition, for promotion and a higher salary, the better car, the foreign holidays? Was it the attraction and influence of ruthless but successful executives who I had worked with over the years?

As we passed the white horse, faintly discernible, etched into the hills in the distance, I made my decision. I picked up my mobile and rang the company in London. I apologised and told them that the train was running far too late to get me there in time and so I was deferring my visit for the time being. The woman on the other end of the line sounded curt but, understandably, not unhappy and I rang off. I finished the rest of my coffee, packed my laptop into its case and stood up to get my jacket as we approached York. I had no intention of going any further. Ten minutes later I was standing on the northbound platform waiting for the next train back to Darlington.

I don't remember anything of the journey back. My thoughts were preoccupied with the boy, his clothes, his ancient fishing tackle and the overall confusion, concern and sense of loss that I felt.

Arriving back in Darlington I collected my car, drove down Victoria Road, turned left at the top and headed for Hurworth Place where I crossed the Tees and parked outside the Croft Spa Hotel. I got out and walked back over the road bridge and down to the river in the direction of the railway bridge. As I walked quickly, almost jogging, I was vaguely aware of my side of the river being a dirty purplish colour which continued as I approached the sandhole where the boy had been. There was no sign of anyone and I'm not sure how I felt. Certainly confused but also relieved, not really surprised and yet I had an overwhelming feeling of disappointment, of what I might have learned. There were no footprints in the soft ground around the sandhole and the dying Himalayan balsam was tall and unbroken. I walked a little further in case he had moved on but there were no signs of anyone having passed that way for some time.

I don't remember much about walking back to the car or getting in it but I knew then that I would have to return the following day at the same time that I had seen him, partly in the very faint hope that he would return but also because I wanted to experience for one more time a fishing day of my youth when the boy existed to try and recreate the feelings and thoughts of that innocent teenager. I drove straight to the Darlington Angling Centre in North Road to buy some maggots after which I intended to go home and dig out the oldest tackle that I could find, I still had the rod that I'd got for Christmas in 1962, and go back to the sandhole the following day to relive my boyhood fishing day. I also still hoped that the young angler might return, but to be honest by this time I felt he must simply have been someone fishing there, who, because of my tiredness, stress and probably my hangover, I had attributed too great a likeness and had over reacted.

The fellow angler behind the counter asked where I intended going as he had heard that the Tees was fishing well with good bags of grayling caught on maggot around Low Coniscliffe which was a few miles upstream of Croft. I told him that I was after chub or roach and intended to fish the stretch below the railway bridge at Croft. He frowned, shook his head and told me that there was no point in that. An industrial cleaning business, north of Darlington, had accidentally released chemical waste into the Skerne a few weeks ago which had killed everything in it. The Skerne ran into the Tees just before Croft and so had polluted it too. The effect, he said, could be clearly seen by the dirty purplish colour of the Durham side of the Tees for miles.

"There's nothing in there," he said. "All the fish have been killed by the pollution and so no one has fished there for over a month – there are signs telling you there's no fishing allowed until further notice."

The following morning I went back to the sandhole around five thirty. This time I didn't even need the alarm clock as my mind had been turning over and over and I had barely slept and had lain awake since three. I carried only a haversack with a spare jumper and flask of coffee in it. I sat for an hour or so huddled in my coat but saw nothing other than a heron which had lifted off from the other bank as I arrived and the occasional rabbit. I waited until the train passed over the bridge at around quarter to seven then reluctantly picked up my haversack and walked slowly back to the car. When I got back to the house I brewed a pot of coffee, buttered a couple of slices of fresh toast, then sat down to write my letter of resignation to the board.

OUR BRIDGE
IAN TODD

We met on the set of Auf Wiedersehen Pet. It wasn't love at first sight. The first time I saw her I thought she was a bit much and an attention seeker. Then we spent some time together waiting for re-shoots and long lunch breaks.

We used to sit down next to the Tees and stare at the Transporter Bridge. I wasn't from the area and it used to fascinate me. I had never seen anything like it. Linsey used to tell me about the bridge, fill in the details and tell me about her childhood adventures.

When we had our first date, I never wanted the night to end. We sat and talked for hours. It felt like we had known each other for ages. It was effortless and fun. She used to have day-trips to Hartlepool and Saltburn. She enjoyed getting lost in the crowds. We used to sit and listen to Mogwai. One headphone in each of our ears, we drifted off into the music. It is a place I often go back to and disappear into the beauty of the moment. This is the place we fell in love.

Months after meeting her, I returned to the region and settled down. I got a job and fell into her world. We used to go to gigs and art galleries. We talked about one day we would get married and travel. When she died, my world collapsed. I know the area often gets derided but for me it is home and I see its industrial beauty. We used to come back to the bridge on our anniversaries.

Maybe you are meant to have great moments in life alongside the boredom and the pointlessness of the everyday. There are always moments of beauty and happiness out there. It's just life has a way of balancing it all out. I know we will never have them moments again. That day in June, my world changed forever. I'm glad I got to have those moments. Some people never have those moments. All we have is photographs and memories now. It is our bridge.

POINTED AND PRECIOUS
EMILY WILLIS

I am struck by how long I seem to be falling. As everything flattens out in front, random things enter my head. The man in the photograph, he'd approached the bar with a certain je ne sais quoi. Now was his moment, this was his bar across which to enchant, checked shirt dipping in the Sambuca. I lined up the scene, thought it would make a great shot, didn't know how to take it without his noticing.

"I'll have twenty-five Apple Sourz. Make sure you put the deal on, yeah?"

"I'm sorry that offer only runs until eleven."

His nose twitched. "What? You gotta be kidding. I could have bought shots an hour ago."

"You could have, but you didn't."

"Whoa." He held up his hands. "There's no need to be like that. I just want to know the reason behind the crazy logic?" His friends were next to him, and the lass for whom he'd been buying drinks.

"Well, I'd imagine it's to get you drunk early so that you buy more later."

"No way! If I walked up to you right now like and stole your tips, I'd be arrested, right? It's the same thing. Come on. I won't tell anyone." Wink wink.

"I'm sorry."

"Let's call it a fiver, between me and you." He dangles it in what he calculates to be an alluring fashion, just out of my reach. (It's one of the old ones that we're not allowed to accept.)

"Sorry I can't."

"Right, I've had enough of this. I want to see the manager."

The lass he was with caught my eye and held it, and for a second she looked like Corrie. She paid for the drinks. When I turned back to give her the change she had disappeared.

He was one of the last ones, and the bouncers were rounding up the stragglers. The lass seemed to have changed her mind and was nowhere to be seen. He was against a pillar, legs kicked out in front of him. Someone had put a bog roll on his head. I got out my phone and, after a moment, snapped him like that, for my portfolio. The contrast was good.

I like to take detours on my way back, heading up Linthorpe and out towards the A19. I get so tired I could actually put my face on the bar, even with Justin Bieber thumping in my ears. But then it hits two, or three, and I go past that. Then I might as well stay out and catch the hours before the sun comes that go the colour where everything loses shape.

It was one of those nights, June clouds through copper sulphate streets, something of Gogh's, a kind of prescience hanging. On the country roads, semimorphous things came pointed and precious out of the night, signs of life that seemed incongruous, they presented themselves; moths like dandelion clocks looming out of bends, smashed to dust. The shapes in the bushes then came through a gold mist – green-eyed hedgehogs with that look of permanent surprise. At this time, there is no point indicating; I accelerated towards roundabouts, felt the pleasure of speed, reward for completing another shift in the place without windows, and for being out late enough to witness this colour.

I turned the music up, something from David Lynch, I'm Waiting Here, and pretended I was in the video, American Midwest roads unfolding and unfolding. The music was fuller than in the day, or I was more permeable, some kind of osmosis took effect, flooding me.

Then there was just the engine straining, and all those fields. Part of me wanted to race back to be within walls, to the sheets that smell of fresh and the arms I wished would be pillow-flung.

Corrie doesn't like me driving out late because of the car, it being on its last legs. I got it a few years ago. Had to save for ages. She's one of those old blue Polos, the shade you don't see anymore. 2000 reg. Had to clean it out at first because it stank of fags. I keep a bottle of engine oil in the boot and top it up every thirty miles or so. I'm hoping not to see any police because of the missing headlight, and there's several warning lights on the dashboard. But, it's mine.

I dip the clutch, pushing into third with just the edge of a finger. I feel my hands more than I've felt them all night, more than that broken glass. I never thought I'd learn to drive because of the way I am – when it happens – but I did. Dad took me out sometimes before the traffic and we'd drive all the way to the dales along the moorland roads banked by heather. I burnt his clutch out once trying to get uphill. In my defence, the bite was poor and who takes a learner on their first outing up Sutton Bank?

Sometimes Corrie, when I work a day shift, says she'll pick me up and I ride on the back of her bike. We go back through the park on the long route to Thornaby. She's quite little and I'm quite heavy so she cycles in slow motion and I am convinced it would be faster walking. I can't see her face but I imagine it is set against each revolution like Sisyphus with his rock, only the terrain, she says, is more hazardous. There's a tonne of potholes and I'm surprised I haven't developed piles. She cycles frog-like, which just about keeps the bike steady and stops us from ending up in the ditch, again. She likes to stop to pick daisies too and thread them through her button holes; she's skilled now, can do it without looking with one hand. Once she picked one covered in turd; the smell wafted towards me and I thought at first there must have been a continuous line of invisible poo somewhere near the path.

Another time, it was dark, and we were going over her recent date in such detail that we missed our house, and kept going for miles, up to the bridge. She took her hands off the bars as we gained speed; the lights, slightly different shades of velvet, separated out and we moved through the lines joining the curve as though through DNA, free-wheeling on past the warehouses.

I could have listened to her advice, gone home and come back the next day. But I didn't want to miss the chance to take the photo. Yet the thought was seeded now, had been hovering for months like the moths: what if it happens again? I've always had this, compulsion, to frame things. But, occasionally, when I see something recondite, like a painting or landscape, I throw up. Or, things start to spin, and, I experience things that never happened.

I fall, for instance. It comes without warning and leaves without me realising. There's a word for what I am: Stendhal's. (Except I haven't marched across Europe with Napoleon, and it doesn't happen when I look at Volterrano's fresco of the Sibyls). It's been happening more and more; I even feel sick in anticipation of the thing. The challenge is to try and take the photos before falling.

Last time, I was at South Gare. There was a jaundiced moon, shot through with remnants of day like cut glass, and her. All angles. She was pale and spider-like as the tread of some undiscovered thing on the ocean bed. Even her lips, cracked pale under her make-up. Only Corrie's hair is soft; it curves in the wind.

She'd brought me there with my camera one night when I wasn't working.

"You'll see why!" Breathless, her lips parted animatedly, and I knew she had found what she was looking for. The boat jolted as she plunged her arm in up to the shoulder, weeds wound away from those strands, and ripples went spilling spilling. She emerged slowly, something silvery and cerebral in her cupped hands.

"Put it down! It'll sting you! Why is it not stinging you?" I shouted from the pier.

She didn't respond but pressed a finger into the cytoplasmic globe; the creature seemed to swell with its own pressure.

"I can see through you," she murmured, holding it up to the night. She kissed the bald smoothness as if it was foetal.

The sound surprised me, more sinuous than watery, as she ripped one of its tentacles. I let out a sound that wasn't me. She looked up.

"It's already dead, you know."

I didn't speak.

"I dare you to eat it."

"What?"

"Go on – eat it, eat it!" She giggled, climbing the steps and running towards me.

I wheeled away. She stopped, regarded me. Then threw the tentacle away and placed the jellyfish unceremoniously on her head. Suitably balanced, I watched what was by turns grotesque and hilarious, as she wiggled her head and the lopsided wig began to dance. A globulous puppet.

She crossed her eyes and stuck out her tongue. "Look, I'm a jellyfish."

The shot was forming. I contemplated the angle, the distance between the pier and water, but the sea and the night have a habit of distorting distance. Although I'd been there before and knew exactly how far down it is, it nevertheless became a depthless place without colour.

When I began to fall I thought of everything all at once tumbled and tumbled gaining speed I would not stop at terminal velocity the air would flay the lips and eyes off me and still I would not have hit the water still have not felt the deadweight cold the sudden under-plunge dragging me out there was no light I couldn't tell which was back to shore and which was out to sea…

When I came around, the sea was surprisingly hard; I could feel gravel. Because of this, I didn't think I was dead, but didn't open my eyes. Instead I flexed my muscles to see if anything felt broken, licked my lips but didn't taste salt.

Then I heard Corrie.

A large gull was contemplating me, head on its side, wide-eyed. Behind, the sea rose over the concrete, swallowing the sky. I understood why crabs walked sideways.

Quite without warning, I turned the car around and drove back, watching lights race towards me and slip into each other. MIMA is a building I always stop to absorb, white stone like quartz, and the shape of the thing, protruding like the prow of a ship, and all made of glass. You could line four people up in these panes and still the span would be broader such that you could still see what went on inside. I enjoyed the way light and rain played fluidly off them at this time, those structuring states; water; light; I wanted them for my pictures. If I could take an iconic shot and use them right, MIMA might display it. Here, I thought, the Bottle of Notes.

Approaching it, there was a snuffling sound. I walked around the edge and saw a woman sitting with her back to it. She was wearing a green-yellow bodycon bunched up around her thighs, and black platforms, bark chips between her toes. She had a small tattoo of what looked like a wave cresting her ankle. Her hair was long, loose around the shoulders, dyed purple-black, and there were thick layers of kohl on her cheeks.

"Are you alright? Are you lost?"

She looked up. Her pupils were enlarged, it made her eyes black, and I remembered her as the lass from the club, the one who'd looked like Corrie. The same flicker of recognition crossed her face.

"No, I just come here sometimes, to…" She paused, searching for the right word.

I saw that she was in the stages of inebriation where the outside air hits you and either propels you into the acrid mess of cold-toilet-bowl-against-face-holes-in-the-reel-of-last-night's-memories-ness, or, the world starts to come back, you get out of your head, notice the autumn bite, angle of street lamps, all the sounds that are suddenly close, and the feeling starts to return. It seemed she was tending towards the latter, so I pulled off my rucksack and retrieved my water and jacket.

She hesitated, wary, then took them and pulled the coat tight.

"So, you were saying, you come here…"

"…to rethink." She nodded decisively. "Yes."

"To rethink?"

"Yes," she repeated, and looked at the floor, prodding a hole in the dirt with a piece of bark.

"I'll be fine," she murmured. "It's just the red wine talking. Red wine and rum!"

"I know! They say they're a lethal combination, the dark substances. If you have a night on white wine and vodka you'll be fine, but rum and red wine in the same quantities… it's an own goal."

"Is that true?"

"Well, I've yet to test the theory… It's on my list, mine and my housemate's."

She smiled.

It was then I noticed how the night was changing, pale fringes shimmering on the edges. I needed to take the photo soon.

"Are you alright?" she asked. "You're… fidgeting."

I told her then, the reason why I come here.

"Of course, I can't come in the day, because the photo needs to get inside the Bottle and for that I need to climb it and they don't like that, understandably, but the media tries to paint us as ignorant of the sacredness of art, but, you see, actually, I think it's good that people climb it, it emphasises the continuity between the cultural fabric of the Boro and the art it produces, it wouldn't feel true if we didn't touch it, something made of steel, when people have been working with their hands their whole lives, it's this encounter with art and history in a very visceral way, and language too, how we climb language every time we try to speak, then there's the very obvious symbolism of art as a form of social support, a social ladder…" I stopped, very aware that I might have bored her.

But she said, "That's fascinating. I'd never thought of it like that." She picked herself up, leaning for a moment against the frame. "I'll move out the way."

I paused, allowing the idea that had been hovering at the edge of our conversation to surface.

"Would you mind if… if I took some with you in? It just wouldn't feel right to take the photo now, because when I came across it, you were here. I'd give you a copy…" I waited.

"How would you take it?" she asked slowly.

I pointed. "From above, like the quote about the gulls. It seems to necessitate a bird's eye view. Things look different from different angles. Then I thought if we could find the words 'the passage of Venus' from Cook's diary, you could stand inside the Bottle, in front of there, then it's like it's not just Cook's words but…"

"Ours," she finished.

I smiled. "Yes."

"I don't know if I'm going to be able to get in… but I'll give it a go." She went feet first, arching, wriggling. "If I get stuck, I'm blaming you."

I walked around, trying to find the script, but the calligraphy was almost illegible.

"I don't think it matters," she said, "if you think about it, now the message is not just Cook's and those artists' but anyone's."

"Yes, yes, I do like that," I said, thinking of mum, and when dad had left to work the Brent she had been so distraught and he'd said, "Write me letters, and I'll store up replies for when I get back. You can have them to read next time." When she'd asked where to address them, he'd said, "The sea." So she'd gone to Coatham every Saturday, before anyone was up, and knelt by the waves with bottles, tightly folded letters and waded in, letting the waves take it. He always said he got them. Even after she'd stopped writing.

I hesitated; now to climb and try not fall or puke (or both). She looked at me through the layers of words, blue and white.

"It's okay," she said.

Taking it slowly, I started climbing, stopping to breathe and check my footholds on each letter. At the top I looked down; the scene was fizzing at the edges. Things were perfectly balanced, the lighting, the shade of the dress against the steel, viewed from above but also from the inside simultaneously. I started to sway, feeling nauseous, gripped the metal more tightly with one hand.

I can see the pulse in my wrist I wrap my leg through a letter anticipating the hallucinations I already know that somewhere amongst these will be the image I want her with her back to me hands clasped around letters looking out through an o or possibly an a adjust the exposure then cover the scene from three sixty degrees the images will form a circle ask her to face the camera she leans back looks straight at the lens it is happening everything flattens and slides the kohl in two lines down her cheeks but she is smiling encouragingly and it lends the moment a double authenticity the bottle and its ponderous contents many faces coming coming towards…

THE SKIRMISH AT YARM
DAVID WILLOCK

York
February 1643

My Dearest Love,

I know that you must be greatly concerned about my welfare. By the time you receive this letter you will already have heard of the engagement that took place at Yarm. Let me assure you, my dearest, that I am well and of good spirit, though I have some small bruising that is of little consequence. I apologise for not having written sooner but my duties have prevented me from doing so and you know all too well what the responsibilities of a captain in my lord of Newcastle's Regiment means. I know that you will be eager for detail of what took place but a few short days previous, if only to reassure you of my words, so I shall not keep you longer.

As you know, my lord Cavendish was assigned the task of getting much needed supplies to our fellows in York. They have been sore pressed these last months and in need of some relief. It was for this reason that a column of supply was organised under the joint command of Lieutenant-Generals King and Goring. It was only natural that I should be assigned to travel with them. As it turned out, the entire regiment went south, which was just as well as you will soon see.

We made good distance and in good time. Even though the roads, made hard by the winter chill, soon turned again to mud under the weight of tramping feet and laden wheels, each in turn ploughing what snow there was into the broken earth. The weather, though bitter and cold, did not hold up our progress. We have been fortunate that the snows, so common at this time of year, were not falling. We took this as a good sign as we approached the village of Egglescliffe on the River Tees, and the first of the few bridges that allowed for a crossing. Being late in the day the majority of the force camped some distance away so as not to alarum the local populace.

While the men sought shelter in the fields around the village, many of my fellow officers were quartered in Stockton Castle, a few miles hence. Camp fires were permitted and, while we did consider that they may give away our position and numbers, they were necessary and kept only of sufficient size as to keep the men warm through most of the night. It was a cloudless night. A star strewn heaven which, on a warm summer day is a beauty to behold, heralds nothing but a bitter chill. A hard night for any man abroad to find repose at this time of year.

There had been reports of scouts in the fields and woods around us as we travelled south but in truth I cannot swear to have seen any. Doubtless this was due in no small part to the dragoons that were ordered to ride our flanks and protect us from surprise and enquiry. If there had indeed been scouts, trying to hide our numbers would have been a pointless exercise and one that would have had great effect upon the morale of the men who, without the fires, would shiver through the dark hours.

I did not spend the night with my fellow officers and I know you will be wondering why. All will soon become clear, dearest heart, so please be patient. I spent some time with my men before retiring. They spoke of home, of family. It was clear that many missed their wives and children. To avoid melancholia there began a series of impromptu songs, the words of which I dare not record here, my darling wife, for they are not of the sort that ought to be allowed to taint the ears of women of your gentile station. For all their impropriety, they did serve to keep the spirits of the men high so I believe the Lord God will forgive them of their trespasses. My last words to them, before I left to sleep, were instructions on how we were to conduct ourselves the next day and to keep clear heads. My last words were aimed at Jack Price, the miller's son from Blythe. I cannot say for sure what he carries in his canteen but I do know that he is less well behaved after drinking regularly from it. I guess we must all find our courage from somewhere at times like these.

You will know all too well how hard I find it to sleep before an action. On this night I could not ask my men to suffer the bitterness of the night, followed by the consequences of the day, knowing that I had slept comfortable in a warm bed, in a cosy room. My men deserve better. I was sorely tempted to wander the camp ground until the sun came up, but I did not want to give the men alarum. So I attempted to doze in my tent and when that did not work I took to reading. I know there are some that think I pack too much for a journey such as the one we were making but the books I carried with me were a comfort, and they served to pass the time. At some point I must have embraced Hypnos for I was awakened by Billy Cutpurse just as the sun was breaking the horizon. My first prayer of the day was the hope that my men had found time for a little sleep too.

The first day of February dawned with a thick, low lying mist filling the hollows, crevices and valleys that mark the landscape in this part of the world. The rising sun cast an ethereal light that surrounded us. Strange shapes there were in that mist. Trees that had weathered into grotesque shapes came to life at this moment, in the eyes of the mind. At times man was mistaken for wood and wood for man. It was through this unearthly mist that I saw General King approach. He appeared from the misty shadows, along with his entourage, as if he had risen up out of the very ground. A passage from the Bible you gave to me before the column left Newcastle, and that I read each night before I sleep, came to mind:

...and the voice cried behold, and I looked and I saw a pale horse, and he that sat on him was death, and hell followed with him.

General King greeted me then and stopped to have words with the men. They were rousing words and I could see the pride reflected in the eyes of each man when General King had finished and moved off to be swallowed by that same mist that had hidden his initial approach.

We readied ourselves then, for the day's work was still ahead. I must say that seeing the men so gathered they did appear as apparitions in their white coats and hats in that grey swirling mist. Would that they did so appear to our enemies for it would have struck fear into the hearts of many and make the crossing of the Tees less dangerous.

We were to be aided in our efforts this day by the Rector of Egglescliffe, a man called Isaac Basire. What I hear of Master Basire he appears to be a good man, devout in his commitment to God and King. Though he be a shadow of a man in his build and appearance, he has the command of anyone that should spend time in his company. He is a very learned man and able to converse on a wide range of subject. You would like him, I think, my dear.

As you will know, the bridge at Yarm has a draw section to the north. It is the responsibility of this good Rector to raise and lower that section each day, a routine that the rebels would be familiar with given how long they have occupied the area south of the river. Though such a routine may have made them less than observant, we were all too aware of what we would face once the draw section was in place. If we were lucky the rebels would take no meaning from the lowering. But we could not trust to luck. If the enemy were warned of our coming, if they were organised and of determined spirit, which they were most certain to be, then many of my fellows would be lost.

Fighting in villages is not like fighting in the open fields, dearest. Where there is space to form the regiment in proper order, the pikes become the primary weapon of attack and defence. In the confines of the village street, such cumbersome weapons can be a hindrance as much as a help. There is of course, always the exception to the rule. A well organised, well disciplined block of pikes can prevent the passage of even the most ardent of soldiers. Form them up at the end of a street, at an intersection or maybe the exit from a bridge and they become a formidable obstacle. To remove them will require courage, determination, strength and the willingness to sacrifice enough men to clear the way, though the pikes do become vulnerable to the fire of muskets.

This then was what greeted us after the drawbridge had been put into place and we could survey the far bank of the River Tees. The exit to the bridge was blocked by companies of muskets, behind which columns of pikes stood ready to bar our way and defy our horse if we were to get too close. Bristling like the spines of a hedgepig, each sharp tip pointed towards us, the pikes of the rebels challenged us to cross; tested our courage and resolve with their silent confidence as they stood, rank upon rank, waiting for the next move in this dance of death.

Oh dilemma upon dilemma, my dearest! What were we to do? If we tried to rush them, their muskets would give way to the pikes and we would find ourselves at a disadvantage of arms, for we could not rush with pike. If we stand and trade shot, the bridge would soon become clogged with our dead and wounded, making the crossing even more perilous.

Alas, there was nothing for it but to gird ourselves manfully and press forward. At that moment, the moment when my men and I were about to set foot upon the perilous journey, a galloper was brought into place. The men of the ordnance, harassed by rebel dragoons, manhandled the piece into position and let loose with a murthering shot that discomforted the rebels greatly. No longer were their muskets barring our way. The best that the rebels could do was plug the gap with their pikes, but it was to no avail. We took the fight to the enemy and with carouselling musket fire, did them great damage and injury.

We had approached to within fifty yards when I gave the call to charge forward. In an instant a hundred men leapt forward and gave the fight to what was left of the defenders. They could not stand ere long and began to give ground. Further we pushed forward and in no time we were free of the confines of the bridge's parapets.

The fighting was fierce and through it all I swear that I could hear our drum beating out a frantic rhythm. Billy Cutpurse earned his money this day.

Soon there was the sound of hooves on cobbles as our horse chose their moment to enter the fray. The rebels could take no more and threw down their weapons in an effort to escape. Running in all directions they fled the field, though for many it was an effort in vain. As you will know, my dear, from all that we have talked about, the greatest number of casualties are taken as the fight nears its end, when the blood is up and the lust to deal death is at its most powerful.

We managed to capture the enemy baggage train and the usual pillaging took place. There was much additional plunder to be had in arms, armour and supplies that would go to the garrison at York. Personal items taken from the dead and captured disappeared without a trace. Sadly it was obvious the rebels had not been paid recently for there was little coin to be had, even amongst their wagons.

For all the fierceness with which the day began, the encounter did not last long. Indeed it could be called nothing more than a skirmish. The number of dead and injured was slight, at least amongst ourselves. Though there is one such casualty that I must report to you with a saddened heart, my dearest. It is that of the orphan boy Billy Cutpurse. He had too few years in this life and I pray the good Lord will take him into His keeping. While I feel the discomfort of his loss, I am more moved at the thought that he was not killed on some foreign campaign, but in the fields of England, by Englishmen! I am forced to ask what the future can be for a country where they have fallen to killing their children. Though I know our cause is just, in defence of the anointed king, I fear that you may be right, my darling wife. It may just be that, as your favourite playwright Mr Shakespeare has said, there is a pox on both our houses. If it is so then none shall prove the victor because of it. Nevertheless, we are engaged in a great struggle and must see it through to its end.

The regiment are due to return to Newcastle in a few days and I shall be glad to be once again in your loving arms, my dearest. Please let my sons know I miss them and long to be with them. Kiss my daughter for me and let her know that I shall be home soon. Until then and for always I shall remain your loving husband,

Rupert

A note from history:

This story is fictional. Though there was indeed a skirmish that took place across the bridge at Yarm, there is no record of exactly what happened, only that the Royalist forces were victorious and the much needed supplies reached York. The contemporary Royalist publication 'The Mercurius Rusticanus' does record that the number of the enemy was four hundred foot, three troops of horse and two pieces of ordinance. No mention is made of the size or composition of the Royalist forces, though it is fair to assume that it was considerable as the command was divided between two generals.

Along with the official accounts of the events of the English Civil War, there are numerous personal accounts too, giving a different view on events. In writing this piece I considered what someone who might have experienced the event would record for the benefit of others.

As with all historic fiction based in fact, some of the characters are real. Lieutenant-Generals King and Goring were indeed commanded to get the supplies to York and the Rector of Egglescliffe, Isaac Basire DD did have the responsibility of raising and lowering the draw bridge. He was also chaplain to King Charles I.

William Cavendish, Earl of Newcastle (contrary to many of the contemporary records of the encounter, William Cavendish was not created Marquis until 27th October 1643), had responsibility for, and command of, the northern counties for the King. His white coated regiment earned a fierce reputation during the opening phases of the English Civil War, but they ceased to be a force to be reckoned with after they were decimated at the battle of Marston Moor in July 1644. It is reported that only thirty men, out of a compliment of around twelve hundred, survived the assault on them by dragoons as they occupied the ground known as White Sykes Close near to the village of Long Marston, after they had repulsed repeated attacks by Parliament cavalry. All other names are a creation of my own and do not represent any actual person.

WRITER IN RESIDENCE CONTRIBUTION

ECLIPSED
TRACEY ICETON, WRITER IN RESIDENCE

I'd just clambered up the stepladder to count the tinned tongue when the shop bell tinkled. I hopped down a step, cursing that Boche sniper, his bullet now ten years lodged in my knee.

The kitchen door banged open. Alfie rushed through, the tea tray shaking in his scrawny hands. I jolted down another step; the ladder wobbled perilously.

"I'll go, Mr Chadfield," he offered, a full eight stone of lemony keen pep.

"Aye, save me, lad. Mind, it'll be Mademoiselle…"

"Don't worry, Mr Chadfield, I'll see to it." He rushed through, still carrying the tea tray.

With a grimace, I hauled myself back up the ladder. Lad was like a pup training to herd sheep; scampering about, tail a-wagging, scattering ewes haphazard like. Still, he'd settle down. I started tallying the tins.

Gallic words swanned through to me. "I have come for the order."

Instead of Alfie's chipper chirruping there was just the rattle of cups in saucers; I pictured the tea things shaken to life, Alfie stood struck mute as midnight. Would've been better if I'd gone myself. Damn Boche. Hobble. Hop. Hobble. As I landed on the tiled floor Alfie found his voice.

"Or-order?"

"Oui. Monsieur Chadfield prepares it every week. I collect first thing."

"F-first thing?"

"Oui, le pain, le beurre, le fromage, le lait, les oeufs…"

"Les who?"

"Alfie," I called, "I'll serve Mlle Rousseau."

I scuffed across the stockroom.

"Les oeufs, eggs."

"Oh, e-eggs." There was a rattle, Alfie setting the tea things down.

"I'm coming, Alfie," I called again, the doorway three teeth-gritting steps away.

The noise was like a cat scrabbling to escape a cardboard box. Then a clatter. Then the scream.

"My coat!"

I found Alfie, face redder than a raspberry, sprawled across the counter, clutching an empty egg tray. The floor the other side of the counter was egg-splatted; slimy whites, gooey yellows, shell-shards. Dead centre of bombardment was Charlotte Rousseau, an exquisite statue spattered with hens' farts, goop trickling down her crimson coat, one egg plopped on her matching beret.

"Clumsy oaf," she cursed, dark ringlets quivering. "My coat, c'est ruined."

"Mlle Rousseau, let me help." I rushed to her. "Fetch a cloth, lad."

"Y-yes, Mr Chadfield."

I whipped out my hankie, dabbed at Mlle Rousseau's coat, throwing Alfie a, 'quick-smart-or-you're-for-the-plank,' stare. But he couldn't see owt 'cept the French belle, fantasy fast steaming up his brain.

"Now!"

He shook himself to and scarpered.

"Who is he?" Mlle Rousseau sniffed.

"My new assistant."

"Useless boy," she proclaimed.

"Overeager," I excused. "Him and his mam've only been here a fortnight. Come from down south. His dad passed away…" I hoped the sob-story would soften her. "…they moved to be near his mam's folks in Stockton. She made posh frocks for a London outfitters: couture, like. She's working at Blacketts now." I was gibbering but the Rousseaus were my best spenders. "Reckon she'll fix that for you no bother." I pointed at Mlle Rousseau's hat.

Finger by finger, she teased off a kid glove, gracefully raised an elegant hand to her head and patted, with scarlet-tipped fingers, her egg-sopped titfer. Cold, gluey egg snot slicked her skin. She inspected her slimed hand, petite nose wrinkling and sapphire eyes frowning at the eggy gunge.

"Pah! I go to change." She brushed me off, drew tighter

the belt that cinched in her tiny waist and turned on her heeled patent leather shoes.

"I'll deliver the order for your mama later," I called, words slammed in the door, bell jangling angrily.

Alfie reappeared. His carrot top curls were slicked down. His collar was done up; his tie straightened. He waved a grubby cloth triumphantly.

"She's gone."

He slumped. "I was looking for the coal tar soap."

"I don't keep it by the mirror," I said, ruffling his hair. "Now see to that lot." I thumbed to the egg-slicked floor. "I don't want anyone going arse over elbow."

Alfie sniffed deeply, sucking up the cloud of rose water Mlle Rousseau had left.

"Does she... come in often?" He spoke in a church whisper.

"Every Thursday."

"She's very..." Words, and sense, slipped from him.

"French?"

Alfie sighed, clutched the mucky cloth to his chest and murmured, "French."

"Now, lad, don't be getting daft ideas," I warned. "She's a canny couple of years older than you. Anyway, I heard she's courting. After marrying money."

"That's alright," Alfie said. "I can put a bit by, now I'm working for you, Mr Chadfield."

"You'll have to do more than that, lad. The Rousseaus were French gentry. Had servants back home. That's why she comes in early, I reckon; picking up shopping's beneath her. Lost everything during the war. Fled here in '17. Funny coincidence, that."

"How so, Mr Chadfield?"

"It's right when I was shipped out there. Second Battle of Aisne, outside Reims. Probably our ships passed in the channel." My hand strayed to my leg. "It's where I got this knee. Now, mop!"

An hour later he was still swishing that mop about like bleeding Cinderella when Daisy Millar called for her mam's usual. He sloshed water over her well-worn boots.

"Alfie, lad!"

"Sorry, Mr Chadfield. Sorry, miss, I didn't see you."

"It's alright. They'll polish. Again." She smiled at him, slipping off her spectacles. "And haven't I said to call me Daisy?"

Alfie wasn't listening. He just twirled the mop and gaped outside. I watched Daisy watching him, her freckled cheeks flushed.

"We've had Mlle Rousseau in," I explained.

"Oh." Daisy's smile wilted. "How's your knee, Mr Chadfield?"

"Fine, love."

She tucked mousy hair behind her ear. "How's your mam, Alfie?"

Alfie muttered some jibberish.

"I'll away to the Rousseau's with this lot," I declared. "Daisy, could you spare a minute, in case there's a rush?" I looked at her, then nodded towards Alfie.

"Of course. I'll do the floor. Men're rubbish at cleaning," she teased, reaching for the mop, her fingers brushing Alfie's.

He kick-started, spluttering, "I'll take the order, Mr Chadfield!"

He was on his bicycle, groceries piled in the basket, before Daisy or I could blink. We watched him pedalling furiously, so focused on the bridge over the river to the Rousseau's that he almost knocked down a young man striding back across from that direction. The chap jumped aside, trilby jarred askew, shaking his fist at Alfie. Daisy turned away, started scrubbing the pattern off the floor.

Alfie damn near wore a rut in that bridge. It was me telling him about Mlle Rousseau's high-falutin' notions over running errands; he'd arrive early on Thursdays, wearing his Sunday jacket, and pedal across with the order before I'd turned the sign to 'open'. There was always something extra, just for her; wild flowers, an embroidered hankie, the slice of fruit loaf from his bait, home-brewed wine, even bon-bons he paid for himself. Worse was when she graced us in person. He'd flap, a chicken cornered by a vixen, torn between rushing out to comb his hair and staying to wait on her. He was too moony to notice how Daisy's normally tack-sharp mam suddenly came over scatty, the poor lass popping in every day for some 'forgotten' thing.

"And not another 'til 1999," Mrs Millar said. "Imagine, nearly the next century before it 'appens again."

"And we'll get the best view of it," Daisy said, nodding to Alfie.

"Place'll be lousy wi' southerners though," Old Mr Johnson moaned. "They're laying on extra trains."

"There's not a bed to be had from Seaham to Bedale," Mrs Vincent bragged.

It was the last Monday in June. For weeks folks had been ablaze with eclipse talk. These three old gas bags had been blethering for twenty minutes just this morning, to Daisy's delight.

"They say it's amazing," Alfie added. He'd taken nicely to chatting up the regulars. Those who weren't so bonny they tied his tongue in knots.

Daisy beamed at Alfie, "Are you going to…?"

"What is amazing?"

It was warm so I'd propped the door open; Mlle Rousseau had slipped in, unseen. We all looked to her now. A breeze fluttered her satin print frock. She slid down her dark glasses, blinking sparkling eyes.

Alfie sprang round to her side of the counter. "The t-total eclipse of the sun."

I saw Daisy remove her spectacles. "Alfie, are you…?"

"Oui. I read about it. We will have a good view?" Mlle Rousseau pouted.

"B-brilliant," Alfie declared, "I'm going to w-watch on the r-riverbank. There's a good spot near y-your house. You c-could join me…if you like."

Daisy replaced her spectacles.

"Mais oui." Mlle Rousseau clapped silk-gloved hands. "It is so romantic. The sun and the moon fitting together, two halves of a heart."

She sashayed out with a generous quarter of crystallised fruit that Alfie weighed for her. He gawped after her. Daisy's bottom lip went trembley. Over the road a young man doffed his trilby to the mademoiselle. Alfie noticed nowt.

"Mr Chadfield, can I take my lunch?" His cheeks flushed.

"Aye."

He was gone ten minutes; came flying back in, a slip of paper crumpled in his hand. Thankfully the shop was empty.

"Mr Chadfield, would you sign this?" He gabbled the question and thrust the paper under my nose. "Please, sir."

"What is it, lad?" I smoothed the creased slip and read the scrawled details. It was from Goldsmiths.

"It's to say I can afford the payments," he panted. "I've got the deposit. It's only a few shillings a week."

"For fifty weeks," I noted. "Now, Alfie, I don't…"

"Please, Mr Chadfield. This is my chance. You heard Char… Mlle Rousseau. The eclipse, Mr Chadfield. If I ask her then she'll say yes, I'm sure."

"That's the plan?"

He nodded. His whole body seemed to glow. I signed, thinking it'd come in handy eventually.

"Thank you, Mr Chadfield." He darted from the shop, pelting along in the direction of the jewellers.

The ring bulged in his trouser pocket the rest of that day, a velveteen box of hope. He didn't show it me but I caught him a couple of times, holding it up to the sun, twirling it 'til the tiny diamond glittered, shot through by sunlight.

Folks wanting provisions for their eclipse shin-digs that night kept us busy Tuesday morning. Rushed off our elbows, we were, and Alfie near useless working one handed; the other kept busy clutching the lump in his pocket.

Midday Mrs Millar came back, Daisy trailing behind.

"That lad wants his ears boxing," Mrs Millar declared, dumping a bag of cornstarch, block of cheese and three carrots on the counter. "How'm I supposed to make my eclipse cake with this?"

"Mam, I'm sure he didn't..." Daisy pleaded.

"He's got some'at on his mind," I said, parcelling up flour, eggs and butter.

"He wants to keep his..."

A thunderous crash bounced through from the stockroom. Mrs Millar tutted. Daisy sighed. I pushed the parcel across the counter, nodding at Daisy. "Might never happen, love."

Daisy tried to smile back. "Come on, Mam." She tugged her mother away.

Out back Alfie was stood at the foot of an avalanche of tinned peaches. I hobbled over.

"Sorry, Mr Chadfield."

"Just clear it up. We'll have to knock summat off any dented tins."

He nodded. The shop bell dingled. I turned to go.

"Mr Chadfield?"

"Yes, lad?"

"When you were in the war did you learn to… speak… French?"

"A bit."

Impatient knuckles rapped on the counter. I glanced at Alfie, hand in his pocket again, away in a fairytale. There was nowt 'cept to leave him there.

"Coming."

It was ten that night before I locked up. We could've served longer but my knee was giving me gyp and I was sick of Alfie's head snapping around like it was on twanged elastic every time the bell dang. I flicked off the lights. Someone brayed on the door.

"Come on, lad. Out the back tonight."

We stepped into the yard. The moon was up, preening itself ready for the big day. Alfie gazed at it.

"G'night, lad."

We stepped into the ally.

"Mr Chadfield?"

"Yes, Alfie?"

"Will you watch the eclipse?"

"Aye."

"So y-you'll be there?"

"Aye."

Silence fogged us. I waited.

"H-how do you say 'will you marry me?' in French?"

I patted his shoulder. "English'll do you, lad."

I was just a few hobbles from home when I saw two figures strolling ahead, arms linked. Mlle Rousseau's shapely silhouette sashayed along, her beret leaning towards the trilbied head beside her. It would come right, I knew.

Next morning the town was up early. Or hadn't been to bed. Drawing the curtains, I saw kids skipping, revellers dancing drunkenly, mams pram racing, old folk quick-stepping. Most carried flasks or picnic baskets. One chap had a loaf under his arm and a tankard in each hand. I remembered witnessing another exodus: Reims, 1917 and the bonny French lass, trudging head bowed, who I'd given my last bar of chocolate. I'd spent that light show ducking the whiz-bang marked 'Chadfield'. War and Love. This time I'd be spectator; it was Alfie's encounter. I flexed my knee, the joint rasping like a rusty hinge.

Ten minutes later I limped my way over the river to where people had clambered up the far bank, waiting to be 'eclipsed'. Cresting the bank I spotted Alfie further along. He was in his Sunday suit, a shabby brown rig-out. Beside him stood Mlle Rousseau, chic in sky blue silk. Alfie had perched up the incline so he was almost on her level. He leaned over to her, pointed at the sky then something in his hand. Was that it? She raised a smoked glass viewer to her eyes. No. I tracked her gaze to where the moon had shoved in alongside the sun, a cheeky pretender in the heavens. I looked back at them. If the moon could conquer the sun, mightn't Alfie win over Mlle Rousseau? Then I noticed the tall young man in the trilby three paces to her right. Clouds gathered overhead.

The crowd shushed. The moon inched closer to the sun. Alfie sidled up to Charlotte. The moon pecked the sun on the cheek. Alfie reached into his pocket. The moon nibbled at the sun. Alfie pulled the velveteen box from his pocket. The moon started to gobble at its paramour, throwing down a triumphant crescent shadow. Alfie faced Charlotte, his hand hovering by hers. The clouds loitered in the wings. The moon gorged on the sun, casting its love spell, devouring the sun. Darkness engulfed the opposite bank, started crossing the river. Alfie dropped to one knee, holding up the velveteen box as darkness galloped towards us. The moon reached its zenith. The spellbound crowd watched for the corona, that gold ring sealing a celestial union. The sun said no; called for the curtain. The clouds fell. The performance ended. We pined in drab darkness for twenty seconds. The jaded moon slipped from its lover's embrace. Sunlight recrossed the river. I limped over to Alfie. He was still on one knee. The sun's rays lit up the bank, lighting on Mlle Rousseau in the arms of the trilby-wearing gent.

I grabbed Alfie's jacket, hauling him up before anyone saw.

"Never mind, lad, there's always next time."

"N-next time? That's not for seventy-two years," Alfie moaned.

"I wasn't meaning the next eclipse, lad. Come on, Daisy'll be in for her mam's order later."